India—land ... ood
dreams! Whe...aths
her her fathe...she
longs to make it her home. But ...s as
welcoming as the Maharaja . . .

Melissa's dramatic confrontation with the daring dia-
mond-thief Sher Singh only strengthens her resolve to
stay. *No one* is going to deprive her of what is rightfully hers. But who is the elusive bandit? And why has he
chosen her land for his hideout? To Melissa, alone in
India in 1883, it seems there is no one—not even the
British Authorities—whom she can trust.

Lynne Brooks spent much of her childhood in northern India. She now shares a rambling country cottage in Dorset with her husband, who is an architect, and a mynah bird. Most of her writing is done during the spring which she spends on a houseboat in Kashmir.

MISTRESS OF KOH-I-NOOR is Lynne Brooks' first Masquerade Historical Romance.

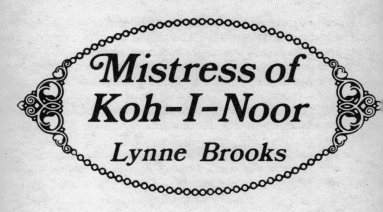

Mistress of Koh-I-Noor

Lynne Brooks

MILLS & BOON LIMITED
London · Sydney · Toronto

First published in Great Britain 1984
by Mills & Boon Limited, 15–16 Brook's Mews,
London W1A 1DR

ISBN 0 263 74557 0

Set in 10½ on 11½ pt Linotron Times
04/0284

*Photoset by Rowland Phototypesetting Ltd
Bury St Edmunds, Suffolk
Made and printed in Great Britain by
Cox & Wyman Ltd, Reading*

CHAPTER
ONE

'Look, Melissa!' Anne Morrison pointed excitedly to the horizon. 'Can you see it? There it is, at last!'

They were standing side by side at the ship's railings, watching the pale fingers of dawn push away the last remnants of night. In the pink glow of the early morning, the sea was calm and the white seagulls screeched and swooped across its pearl-grey waters. The air was warm, warmer than Melissa had ever breathed.

For a moment she closed her eyes, her throat constricted with emotion.

India!

There it lay on the distant horizon, no thicker than a black pencil line. India, at last! The land of so many childhood dreams, of her father's life—and death. It was a land her father had called home. Would it— *could* it—ever be hers?

John Morrison came up on deck to summon them down for breakfast. 'We will not have time to eat in Madras,' he said anxiously, 'the train for Metapilly leaves at noon.' Melissa smiled up at him but shook her head silently, not trusting herself to speak. She knew she would not be able to eat a single morsel now if her life depended on it!

Anne squeezed her hand understandingly. 'Come

on, John,' she said briskly to her husband, 'we will go down and strap our trunks and also have some breakfast. Melissa can stay here if she wishes until the ship sails into port. I dare say we can arrange for some food for Melissa on the train.'

Melissa kissed Anne on the cheek impulsively. How kind and understanding the Morrisons had been! She could not have wished for more affectionate chaperons on so long a journey. Now, with their destination in sight on the horizon, wild horses could not have dragged her away for a single moment!

The deck of the *Centaur* was beginning to fill with excited, noisy passengers. All around was the hectic activity that marks the end of a long journey. Cabin trunks were being hauled to and fro and everyone was rushing around looking for someone or something. Stewards scurried up and down staircases performing last-minute duties, being pulled in all directions at the same time and looking very harrassed indeed.

But for Melissa, nothing existed except the dark line thickening on the horizon as the vast, unfamiliar sub-continent inched itself out of the sea and towards them. The sun's rays were beginning to melt away the wisps of distant mist. Already, she could discern the faint outlines of a white beach spiked with green coconut trees. Melissa clenched the rails tightly, her eyes fixed and unwavering, her thoughts in turmoil.

For a moment she again felt the familiar pangs of panic. Where was she going? What on earth was she doing a million miles, a thousand light years away from her beloved England? Would she ever again see the familiar fields and farms of Cornhill? Or the well loved faces of her friends? She had left behind everything that she held dear in life . . . kindly Mr Winterton, her dead father's friend and solicitor, who had been the instrument of fate in making this impossible journey possible; dear Mrs Rutherford, difficult and demanding as an employer, but so kind on occasion; even poor Basil Smithers, the dull but well-meaning curate in Cornhill who had offered her marriage; Miss Arabella Fenton, at whose Academy she had spent so many happy years . . .

The sudden wave of panic made Melissa shiver a little although the morning air was warm. But then, the panic subsided just as unexpectedly as it had arisen. The coastline ahead was very flat indeed. Beyond the distant white strip of beach she could already discern a row of houses. There was very little vegetation to be seen except on a distant range of low hills.

Melissa watched eagerly, fascinated by everything she saw. This then was the very sight that had greeted her father when, at the age of nineteen, he had first landed in India almost twenty-five years ago in 1858, barely a year after the Indian Mutiny had rocked the country. It was here in Madras, the port towards which the *Centaur* was now heading, that the young Lieutenant Guy Castlewood had met and fallen desperately in love with the ravishing Lavinia Lawrence. They had married within a month of their first meeting. Melissa had been born prematurely barely a year later and, in the course of entering the world, had, in all innocence, claimed the life of her young mother.

Heartbroken, Guy had been forced to send his infant daughter back to England in charge of a kindly family. Through the good offices of his dearest friend,

Clarence Winterton, Melissa had been placed in an excellent institution run by Miss Arabella Fenton, where she had spent eighteen years of her life. It was not until she was almost five years old that Guy Castlewood had been able to visit England to see his only child.

Between the two, father and daughter, had sprung up an abiding devotion, possible only between people who have been deeply alone. Since that first visit, Guy Castlewood had returned to England only twice, but with each visit he had brought into Melissa's young life a little more of the magic of the East. Her heart had filled with pride that this tall, bronzed soldier with so many medals on his chest, was her own, her very own Papa. Oh, how the other girls had envied her at Miss Fenton's!

She had not been able to understand very much about her father's work so many thousands of miles across the sea. But she knew that he was on special leave of absence from the Army to work as tutor to the young prince of the Indian state of Altabad, and that he lived in a very large and beautiful mansion belonging to the Maharaja of Altabad, called Koh-i-noor. She remembered having laughed out loud at the strange sounding name, wanting to know where it had come from.

'Koh-i-noor,' Colonel Castlewood had explained to his daughter, as they strolled arm in arm through Kew Gardens one autumn afternoon, 'is the most famous diamond in the world. It was presented in 1850 to Her Majesty Queen Victoria and is now part of the crown jewels. This beautiful gem came from the diamond mines near Altabad.'

'And what does Koh-i-noor mean, Papa?' she had asked excitedly, awe-struck that her father should live in a house that bore the same name as one of the Queen's jewels.

'It means in Urdu,' he had said, 'a mountain of light.'

The name had captured her childish imagination to such an extent that tears had sprung into her eyes as she clung to him and begged, 'Can I not go back with you, Papa, to your beautiful Koh-i-noor? *Please*, Papa?'

Colonel Castlewood had sighed deeply, fighting back his own tears. 'India is a magnificent country, my darling Missy,' he had said, using his special name for her, 'and one day we shall be together again, I promise you. But it is also a land with many pitfalls for the unwary European. More than anything else, I wish for you to complete your education in England and become a perfect English lady like your dear mother was. After that, I shall bear you away to my Koh-i-noor and we shall be together always.'

She had never seen him again. A few months after he had sailed away again, she had been taken into Miss Fenton's private sitting room at the Academy. 'My child,' Miss Fenton had whispered brokenly, 'you must be brave, very brave . . .'

Soon after his return from England, Guy Castlewood had succumbed to an attack of the dread disease of cholera . . .

It had seemed like the end of everything. The terrible despair that only a child can feel, had engulfed her for weeks, months. She had been only twelve years old at the time. In the past nine years since then, Time, the inexorable healer, had whiled away the wounds and the memories had paled until they lingered only as soft fragrances left behind by a half forgotten dream.

With the help of dear Mr Winterton, who continued to watch over her with care, she had, at the age of eighteen, gratefully accepted the home and position of companion offered by Mrs Lydia Rutherford in a village called Cornhill near Exeter, for Guy Castlewood had left very little money. In many ways, Mrs Rutherford had been a compassionate employer. But, on the whole, Melissa's life had been dry and devoid of joy, with little else to look forward to except, perhaps, a dismal marriage of convenience to Basil Smithers . . .

Melissa felt a gentle pressure on her arm and, with a start, awoke from her reverie to find Anne standing next to her.

'Take your time, my dear,' Anne murmured with characteristic understanding, giving her hand a squeeze. 'John is getting our traps together. It will be another hour at least before we are allowed to disembark.'

'Perhaps I should help . . .' began Melissa hastily, but Anne stopped her with a gesture.

'It's a job best done by a man,' she said firmly, knowing well the emotional turmoil in Melissa's mind. 'You stay here and enjoy the view of your new homeland.' Following Melissa's transfixed eyes to the approaching shoreline ahead, she remarked with a light laugh, 'Very different to your Cornhill, is it not?'

The *Centaur* was now surrounded by the strangest

looking catamarans bobbing up and down in the sea. Melissa watched with growing curiosity; she had never seen such novel looking boats before. Three logs of wood were lashed together to make a raft with the ends turned slightly upwards. Some boats had only one rower, others two. The men, very dark with shaven heads, wore little apart from a cloth around their loins. The boats contained large baskets of fruit and vegetables, obviously for sale to the passengers crowding along the railings. There was much happy chatter with everyone eager to get ashore after more than two months on board.

The Madras harbour was by now very close and Melissa could see several large, pillared buildings, the most handsome of them being, Anne told her, the Customs House. She smiled as she noticed a group of young, excited cadets on board, their carpet bags slung over their shoulders, hardly able to contain themselves in their anxiety to disembark. The catamarans had now been joined by larger boats, a little more sophisticated and polished, with cushioned seats and a canopy, obviously meant to take the disembarking passengers ashore.

'Six months ago,' said Melissa slowly to Anne, 'I would not have believed that I would be standing here now. Indeed, I can hardly believe it at this moment!'

Anne smiled. 'Dear, dear Clarence Winterton! He has been a fairy godfather to you, has he not?'

Melissa nodded silently, her heart too full for words. Anne gave her a sidelong glance, taking in again the flushed pallor of her face and the hint of moisture in her eyes. She hugged her lightly.

'I must run down and see how John is managing. He

does get into a frightful temper if I am not at hand when he needs me.' With a quick smile she hurried below again.

The white beaches of Madras had grown larger as the *Centaur* neared its place of anchor. Beyond them Melissa could see a road along which moved hundreds of tiny, dark figures as they set about their morning duties. Now and then a palanquin appeared, or a bullock cart or even a smart, European carriage. Melissa smiled involuntarily as she considered Anne's remark—yes, it was all very different to the world she had known in Cornhill. A world of comfortable, placid predictabilities, where nothing unexpected happened—until she had received Clarence Winterton's letter on the eve of her twenty-first birthday not six months ago. He had written that he had news of 'serious import' to give her. Her first visit to his office in London the following day—her twenty-first birthday—would be etched in her memory forever, for it had changed the entire course of her life.

'I have received a communication from His Highness the Maharaja of Altabad,' Mr Winterton had informed her solemnly, 'instructing me to give you, on his behalf, a gift of twenty thousand pounds, on this, your twenty-first birthday. Furthermore, His Highness wishes to bequeath to you the house in which your father spent his last years, Koh-i-noor, which is to be yours absolutely as of today.'

The astoundingly generous gifts were being given to Melissa in deep appreciation of her father's many services to the Maharaja and his son, the young Prince, as well as to the State. 'You may not be aware, Miss Castlewood,' Mr Winterton had continued, 'that the young Prince too expired not long after Guy's tragic demise, leaving behind a very young widow and an infant son, a terrible double trauma for the poor old gentleman.'

Melissa had been much distressed at the sad news—and utterly dumbfounded at her own inheritance. Twenty thousand pounds *and* her father's beloved Koh-i-noor! Why, it was more wealth than she had believed existed in the whole world!

'Guy's dearest wish,' Mr Winterton had added quietly, 'was that one day you would make India your home. That, tragically, was not to be, at least not during his lifetime. But, perhaps, even now, a part of your father's dream can still come true . . .'

Melissa had sat speechless, as the full significance of the solicitor's words had struck her. To go to India now, alone . . . a country so far, so alien, even frightening! To leave behind her beloved England, maybe forever . . .

On the other hand, she had argued with herself inwardly, what was her future in England? To spend the rest of her life fetching and carrying for others? Or perhaps, to fritter away her life, alone and lonely, in London, on the benefits of her unexpected windfall? Or maybe, to accept an offer of a depressing marriage to someone like Basil Smithers? Never to taste adventure, never to travel, never to know the world her father had made his own? Even with all the financial independence in the world, what would her solitary existence be worth?

Sitting in Mr Winterton's office that cold, crisp November afternoon, she recalled how long she had argued back and forth with herself. But, at the end of the deliberations, she had been absolutely clear as to which way her decision must lie.

'I will go to India,' she had informed Mr Winterton quietly, 'It is what Papa would have wished.'

Mr Winterton had arranged everything for her, even an introduction to the Morrisons, who lived not far from Altabad. They had been delighted to accept the role of chaperons *en route* to Altabad. And now, on this bright March morning, the end of the long, long journey was in sight.

The *Centaur* blew her sirens imperiously, and sailed with silent majesty into Madras harbour.

The first few hours Melissa spent on Indian soil were dreadfully confusing. So many people, so many strange languages, so much noise—a veritable tower of Babel indeed! The city of Madras, she knew, had been one of the four most important possessions of the East India Company which had, until the Act of 1858, ruled over British India. Even though now the British territories in the country were governed by Parliament through a Viceroy, the Company's erstwhile possessions still enjoyed great importance in the country. Of the four ports the Company had built up for its enormous trading operations—in Bombay, Calcutta, Fort St David and Madras—the last named was considered the most efficient and active although the headquarters of the government were at Calcutta. The British government's military base at Fort St George in Madras was a vital repository of men and armour and the nerve centre of southern British India. Indeed, it was here that the young Lieutenant Castlewood had received his early training when he had first arrived in the country.

It was already past ten o'clock by the time they completed the customs formalities and were allowed to leave the port. The train to Metapilly, John Morrison's district, was due to depart at noon so they were still in good time. Riding in the open carriages to the station, Melissa's eyes devoured everything around, fascinated by the variety she saw. The heat was by now quite intense and, in spite of the parasols they carried above their heads, they were drenched in perspiration.

'Is it always as hot as this in India?' Melissa asked, wiping her forehead with a lace handkerchief.

John laughed. 'No, not always. But we are only twelve degrees north of the equator and it is always humid by the coast.'

'What is the climate like in Altabad?'

'Very pleasant, really. Altabad is 2,500 feet above sea level and is surrounded by forests so the heat is not quite so fierce.'

Melissa heaved a sigh of relief. 'Oh, I am glad. I could not tolerate so pitiless a climate for too long.'

The train journey to Metapilly, which lay in the province know as the Northern Sarkars, was surprisingly cool with a constant breeze blowing through the compartment. The railway track passed over two great rivers, the Penner and the Kistna, and Melissa was enchanted with the panorama of lush flora on either side of the track.

'Altabad has been quite a trouble spot lately because of that wretched man everyone dislikes so— what is his name, dear?' said Anne suddenly in the course of conversation.

'You mean, Chand Ram?'

'Yes. Chand Ram, the Prime Minister of the State.'

'Why is he so disliked?' asked Melissa curiously.

'Because he is violently anti-British and makes as much trouble for us as he can.'

'But surely,' said Melissa, 'the Maharaja is the supreme power in the State?'

'He was,' said John, 'but, unfortunately, since the young prince died, he has aged considerably, I'm told, and leaves matters of State to Chand Ram who is his first cousin and thinks of himself as next in line of succession to the *gaddi*, the throne.'

'But John,' interposed Anne, 'surely the Maharaja's grandson, the late prince's only child, would be next in line?'

'By law, yes,' commented John drily, 'but Chand Ram does not concern himself much with legalities. He will find a way to remove this last thorn in his flesh if he can.'

'Fortunately,' said Anne hastily, noticing the look of horror on Melissa's face, 'the boy was sent away with his mother, soon after the prince died so is quite safe at the moment.' Turning to her husband she said reproachfully, 'You are alarming Melissa unnecessarily, dear. She will think that Altabad is nothing but a den of intrigue!'

'Of course,' said John, instantly repentant, 'I am sorry to have given you a wrong impression, my dear. Anne is quite right. There are many nice people in Altabad who, I am certain, you will enjoy meeting.'

'Who is the British Resident there, John?' Anne asked. 'His name escapes me for the moment.'

'Fred Carstairs. He is a bachelor and rather pompous, but a thorough gentleman.'

'Of course!' Anne said, 'isn't he the one who goes on and on about the North West Frontier policy? If so, he is quite a bore! But, you'll like the Herberts, Celia and George. He is the Chief Medical Officer in the State. Their daughter, Stephanie, is about your age, Melissa, and has just come out from England. Then there are . . . let me see . . . oh yes, Roy and Maree Chandler. Roy is in charge of the diamond mines in Altabad and can be quite entertaining when he's sober. As for Maree . . .' she paused and pursed her lips.

'Maree Chandler?' asked John heartily, 'Now, there is a sight to be feasted upon! She is quite the loveliest . . .' he suddenly caught the glint in his wife's eye and coughed hastily. 'What I mean is, she is, well, she is . . .'

'What he means is,' interrupted Anne acidly, 'that few men in the district can resist her ample charms! She is certainly striking, but much too forward for *my* book.'

John made a weak protest, then laughed. 'The ladies do not care for her,' he said mischievously, 'because she outshines them all at parties!'

'Fiddlesticks!' Anne retorted spiritedly, 'We ladies do not care for her because of the disgraceful dance she leads poor Roy!' She threw John a stern glance and added impishly, 'And, of course, there's Gareth Caldwell . . .' she paused, her eyes twinkling.

'Gareth Caldwell!' John snorted, 'Now, there is a young man I would strongly advise Melissa to avoid scrupulously!'

Turning to Melissa, Anne said sweetly, 'Not a bit, my dear. Now, Gareth is someone the *gentlemen* do not care for because he is not only a crack shot, a superb horseman and a marvellous billiards player, but also the most *attractive* of them all!'

'That has absolutely nothing whatsoever to do with it,' said John stiffly. 'My objection to Gareth bears no relevance to his charms, such as they may be, or to his prowess as a sportsman which, I concede readily, is remarkable. I merely abhor the prospect of a healthy young man doing nothing in life except having a good time.'

'Gareth Caldwell happens to have a private income and therefore can *afford* to do nothing,' said Anne tartly.

'Gareth Caldwell is an arrogant, impudent young pup!' John exclaimed angrily.

'The ladies do not think so,' teased Anne gently, '*especially* your Maree Chandler, if Altabad gossip is to be believed.'

Melissa felt it was time to interpose, not wishing to be the cause of further argument between husband and wife. 'I shall be far too busy with my new home to concern myself overmuch with Altabad society,' she said hastily, then changing the subject, 'How far is Altabad from Metapilly?'

'A little more than fifty miles,' said John, mopping his forehead. 'There is a good road all the way through. I shall be glad to make the necessary arrangements for your journey whenever you wish to leave.'

The sun was just beginning to stir the next morning when the train chugged into Metapilly station with a tired blow of the whistle. John Morrison was Collector of the district, so there was an impressive retinue

of officials and servants to receive him on the platform. The Collector's residence was a delightful,
single-storeyed bungalow washed a pale yellow and
surrounded by a well-kept garden. At the portico they
were again received by a host of smiling servants and
their families, obviously delighted to have the Morrisons back after an absence of a year.

Melissa looked around the bungalow with open
curiosity. It had a verandah running all round and the
rooms inside were dark and cool with high ceilings
and green bamboo screens on the doors to keep out
the hot winds. While John hurried off immediately to
his office not far away, Anne escorted Melissa to the
guest room, giving brisk orders in Hindustani to the
servants. Tired and hot, Melissa longed for a cool
bath and a change of clothing and decided to keep the
thousand questions that came to her mind for a more
opportune moment later. She realised she knew very
little about housekeeping in India and wanted Anne's
advice badly about so many details.

It was not until late afternoon, when they had risen
from a welcome siesta, that John returned to the
bungalow and joined them on the lawn where they
were enjoying a cup of tea. With a tired sigh he
slumped into a bamboo chair.

'A year is a long time to be away,' he commented. 'There are a great many despatches that need re-
plies.'

'No serious problems, I hope?' asked Anne hand-
ing him a cup of tea.

'Just the usual irritations. The revenues have not all
been collected yet, the repairs I had ordered to the
Court House remain uncompleted, we still do not

know when we will receive the telegraph connection from Calcutta . . .' He sighed again.

'Poor dear,' said Anne sympathetically, 'I fear those healthy English roses in your cheeks will soon fade away!'

'Oh and . . . there has been another of those thefts of diamonds from the Altabad mines in the past month.'

Melissa sat up immediately, her curiosity aroused. '*Another* theft?'

'Yes. There has been a series of thefts over the past two years,' he said, 'This latest one, the despatch says, is the biggest haul they have got so far. Most annoying.'

'But who are the culprits? Can they not be apprehended?'

'Easier said than done,' John said with a wry laugh. 'Sher Singh is an unusually clever rascal.'

'Who is . . . Sher Singh?'

'Sher Singh is a damned nuisance—if you will pardon my language! He is a notorious dacoit—outlaw— who has chosen the diamond belt of the Deccan as his hunting ground.'

'I see. Sher Singh . . . does "Sher" not mean lion?'

'Well done!' exclaimed Anne. 'Your Hindustani is improving very fast! Yes, "Sher" does mean lion and he is said to be as fearless as one.'

'He certainly has the nerve of the devil,' said John grudgingly. 'Thank goodness he doesn't choose to operate in my jurisdiction.'

'I know the diamond mines in Altabad are being worked by the British,' said Melissa, 'surely security must be a prime consideration in so valuable a venture?'

'Oh, it is,' said John. 'British troops guard the mines round the clock. But the robberies often take place after the diamonds have left the mines and are on the way to Madras. The feeling is, Sher Singh must have inside information but so far, nobody has been able to discover either his *modus operandi* or, indeed, his hideout.'

'How fascinating!' Melissa exclaimed, thrilled at so romantic a story. 'My father told me that the Altabad mines are among the richest in the Deccan.'

'And among the oldest in the world. Indeed, until diamonds were discovered in Brazil in 1728, India was the world's only source of these gems. Many other Indian mines have "dried out" now, so to speak, but the Altabad mines continue to produce in plenty.'

'The Maharaja must be a very rich man, in that case, since he gets a royalty under his treaty with the British.'

'Oh he is. That is what really irks Chand Ram. He would love dearly to get his greedy paws on those mines.'

'But he can't surely, can he?' Melissa asked, 'without inviting retribution from the British?'

'Oh, he is far too clever for an open confrontation. Rumour has it he is trying to incite rebel activity within the mines as a prelude to eventual take over.'

'Well, I understand little about politics,' Melissa laughed. 'All I know is that I long to see my own Koh-i-noor. Mr Chand Ram is welcome to his diamonds as far as I am concerned!'

'I can understand your impatience, my dear,' said

Anne with a smile. 'John will arrange for a carriage and armed escort whenever you wish.'

'*Armed* escort? Why should I need an armed escort?'

'Because,' explained John, 'the road to Altabad goes through Sher Singh's hunting grounds. And he has been known to hold up private carriages on occasion as well.'

'I do not think that I am going to worry greatly about Mr Sher Singh,' said Melissa lightly. 'Not even he is going to spoil my enjoyment of India.'

'Very well,' said John resignedly, 'I shall make the arrangements tomorrow—but the armed guard, I am afraid, I must insist on.'

But as it happened, John was spared the effort. Early the next morning, a coach and escort arrived from Altabad, sent personally by the Maharaja to take Melissa there. With the coach arrived a maid-servant, Zarina, despatched thoughtfully by the Maharaja to attend to Melissa's needs.

The morning of Melissa's departure dawned dark and thundery. It had rained during most of the night, and the roads had turned into rivers of mud. It was not until noon that the sky began to clear and the roads were pronounced fit for use. The farewells to the Morrisons were tearful. Melissa had been with them now for many weeks and had grown to love them dearly.

'You must be a little careful in Altabad,' said John in a low voice as he helped her into the splendid coach. 'Let me know if you need any help in any way.'

'Goodbye again, dearest friends,' said Melissa hugging Anne, 'and a thousand thanks for all that you have done.'

'And do not forget my offer of assistance,' John urged.

'The most serious assistance I am likely to need,' said Melissa gaily, 'will be in the management of servants who make me very nervous!'

The powerful Arab horses took off in a flurry of flying mud as Melissa waved to the Morrisons until they were lost to sight. There was no way in which Melissa could have known then how very wrong her lighthearted prediction would turn out to be!

As soon as the bungalow disappeared round the corner, she sank back into the luxurious scarlet upholstery, her heart fluttering with suppressed excitement. At last, she was on the final leg of the marathon journey to Koh-i-noor!

The shining, gold-crested carriage sped along the road already drying in the hot afternoon sun. Next to Melissa sat Zarina, small and middle-aged with a plump, smiling face. After the morning's rain the countryside looked marvellously clean. Here and there in the patchwork fields, farmers worked among the tall, swaying stalks of grain, their brightly coloured garments adding vivid splashes of colour to the green of the fields. An occasional snatch of song wafted through the air as lines of women walked along the narrow paths carrying brightly polished brass water pots on their heads. Dotted amidst the fields were clusters of brown, thatched huts with pumpkin creepers climbing up the sides and across the roofs, bearing fat yellow fruit.

It was an enchanting sight and Melissa felt greatly

exhilarated. The steady clip clop of the horses' hooves made her feel pleasantly drowsy. She must have fallen off to sleep, for when she opened her eyes again, the sun was a flaming ball of orange, just about to slip below the horizon. On either side of the road were thick trees, their branches entwining overhead to make a protective arch. As the sun finally disappeared from sight, everything around became dark. Beside her, she felt Zarina shiver.

'What is the matter, Zarina?' Melissa asked.

Zarina pointed to Melissa's silver watch. 'It late,' she said worriedly. 'Dark in jungle not good.'

Melissa smiled and patted her hand reassuringly. 'We have armed escorts,' she said, 'No one will dare to . . .'

She was cut off in mid sentence with the sound of a shot which seemed alarmingly close. She heard Zarina gasp as her own heart lurched.

'Wh-what on earth was that?' she whispered, but Zarina only clutched her arm, her eyes wide with fear. Almost immediately, the carriage ground to a screeching halt. All around them were new sounds of neighing horses and coarse human voices. Outside were loud noises of scuffling and shouting as the torches were extinguished and everything plunged into darkness. Suddenly, Zarina screamed as the coach door was pulled open roughly.

In the flickering light of a match somebody had struck outside, Melissa saw in the doorway, the figure of a man clad entirely in black from head to foot. Two slits in the hood showed a pair of narrow, glinting eyes staring steadily at her. Behind him, in the pale light, she could make out shadowy figures, all dressed in black with their faces concealed behind hoods. Not an inch of flesh showed except for pairs of malevolently gleaming eyes. The figure in the doorway surveyed her silently, then slowly extended a black gloved hand into the carriage. Melissa found herself staring at the barrel of a gun pointing straight at her!

She gave a strangled gasp. 'Wh-who are you?' her voice was a shaking whisper. 'Wh . . . what is it you w-want?'

Without a word, the figure stretched out his other hand, paused for a moment then, quick as a flash, wrenched the silver watch off her dress. The move was so sudden that Melissa could not suppress a scream. As she saw her beloved watch dangling insolently from the black, gloved finger, she felt a sudden surge of anger.

'How dare you!' she exclaimed furiously. 'How *dare* you molest innocent women in this fashion! Give me back my property at *once*, who . . . whoever you may be!'

The figure remained silent, almost mocking, and from beneath the hood she heard the sound of a soft chuckle. The thought that he was laughing at her infuriated her further.

'The watch was . . . given to me by my father, you . . . you *brute*!' she cried, anger bringing tears to her eyes.

Still the hateful black hooded figure said nothing. In another lightning move he withdrew and slammed the door shut. She heard him issue a command in Hindustani and instantly the light was extinguished as the black-garbed figures swung back on to their horses and rapidly melted into the jungle.

For a moment there was a stunned silence. Outside, it was again pitch dark. Recovering her wits, Melissa quickly jumped out of the carriage, followed by a terrified Zarina. Almost immediately, they stumbled over a body on the ground, writhing furiously and making muffled sounds. Fumbling her way around, Zarina knelt down and untied the hands of the attendant who sprang to his feet with a strangled curse and hastily re-lit the torch on the side of the coach. All the attendants, including the armed escort, were lying on various parts of the road, securely trussed and gagged. As they were released one by one, shouting and swearing angrily, they crowded around Melissa obviously concerned about her wellbeing. From what little Melissa could gather out of the confused jumble of voices, one name emerged again and again—Sher Singh!

'I think,' said Melissa finally, 'that perhaps we should proceed with our journey. What has happened has happened and by the grace of God, no one is injured.' She rubbed her bare wrist ruefully. If I ever meet that evil wretch again, she promised herself grimly, I will just show him!

The rest of the journey towards Altabad was tense, but uneventful. By the time they reached the outskirts of the town, Melissa calculated that it must be nearing nine o'clock. Zarina sat slumped in sullen anger, muttering grimly about the lack of alertness of the armed escort that had resulted in the loss of *memsa-hib's* precious watch.

'Don't upset yourself, Zarina,' Melissa said sadly, 'I have enjoyed my precious possession for nigh twelve years. Perhaps this . . . Sher Singh will look after it with as much affection as I have.'

The narrow, winding streets of Altabad town were dark with occasional pools of light from an oil lantern around which people sat chatting. As the carriage passed, they paused and stared at it with undisguised curiosity. Occasionally, Melissa caught a glimpse of a brightly-lit shop filled with tantalising merchandise. She longed to explore but now, more than anything else, Koh-i-noor beckoned!

Soon they left the town behind and the coach took a winding road that climbed upwards. As the night air began to cool, Melissa knew that they must be almost at the top of the hill. The carriage began to slow down, then halted. Glancing out of the window, her pulse beating rapidly as her destination neared, Melissa saw a pair of finely-wrought iron gates looming ahead. The flames of the torches illuminated the royal Altabad crest on the gates, worked out in gold. Slowly and with a creak, the gates opened. The carriage picked up speed again and the horses cantered up a long driveway.

She had arrived at Koh-i-noor!

It was difficult to see very much in the dark but Melissa could discern flowering trees on either side of the road bordering the gardens beyond. Her own land! A wave of incredible emotion swept over her as she breathed in the strong perfumes of exotic night blossoms. The carriage drew up in a brightly-lit portico. The door was opened quickly and, as she stepped out, she saw herself facing a flight of marble steps leading up to the large green doors at the entrance to the hall.

From the shadows emerged a tall, young man in

blue and gold uniform with a scarlet turban on his head. He bowed.

'On behalf of His Highness, the Maharaja, I bid Madam welcome to Koh-i-noor. His Highness is, alas, indisposed, but anticipates with pleasure the opportunity to entertain Madam when he recovers. In the meanwhile, I am commanded to see to Madam's comfort here. My name,' he clicked his heels smartly, 'is Mohan Das.'

Melissa was overwhelmed by the long speech but relieved that it was in English. Before she could reply, however, the coachman, Zarina and the escorts, all began to speak at once. Mohan Das listened for a moment, then his face darkened.

'I am deeply mortified, Madam,' he exclaimed, 'that you should have suffered such indignity at the hands of that villain, Sher Singh. Please accept my humble apologies and . . .'

'Please,' said Melissa wearily, 'let us not talk about it any more tonight. Please be kind enough to convey my warm regards to His Highness and my deep gratitude for his generosity. I look forward to meeting him and pray for his speedy recovery.'

Mohan Das bowed stiffly, then signalled to Zarina to escort Melissa upstairs. 'I have endeavoured to make Madam's apartment as comfortable as possible. Should Madam require anything further, Madam has only to command. The apartment,' he added gently, 'is the same used by Guy *sahib*.' He clicked his heels again, bowed deeply, and was gone.

Slowly, Melissa followed Zarina up the wide, sweeping marble staircase, her eyes moist with emotion. Her rooms—her Papa's rooms!—consisted of a large sitting room opening out into a spacious terrace at one end, a bedroom, dressing room and adjoining bath appointed in black and white marble. The bedroom contained a four-poster bed of carved mahogany with thick royal blue drapes. A lump arose in Melissa's throat. This is where Papa had lived. The lovely mahogany desk in the corner must have been where he sat and wrote those long, loving letters to her at Miss Fenton's. I will not change anything in this room, Melissa determined. I shall keep it exactly as it is.

In the small kitchenette next to the sitting room, Zarina was busy heating the meal that had already been prepared for her. She stepped out on to the terrace. At her feet, bathed in the silvery light of a half moon, lay the vast, sloping grounds of Koh-i-noor. All around were the heady perfumes of the warm, tropical night. Only the insistent chirping of the cicadas disturbed the silence of the night. For a while, she felt very close to her darling Papa, believing with all her heart that he was near, watching over her and wrapping her in the protection of his love.

After dinner, gently spiced and delicious, Melissa realised just how weary she was. The onyx clock by her bedside showed midnight. She unpacked her night clothes and her toilet articles, washed, changed and combed her thick chestnut hair into a neat plait. Then, she slipped into bed, dismissing Zarina for the night.

I should love to stroll through the garden in the moonlight, she thought sleepily. But before she knew it, she had fallen into a deep, exhausted sleep.

CHAPTER
TWO

How long Melissa slept, she did not know, but suddenly she found herself wide awake. For a moment she lay still. What was it that had wakened her? Slowly, she sat up and looked around the room. There was no one there. She got out of bed and went to the window. The world outside was dark and quiet. Even the noisy cicadas seemed to have finally fallen asleep. The moon had set. The only sound she could hear was the soft rustle of leaves rubbing against each other in the night breeze.

She shrugged. Maybe she had been dreaming. As she started to climb back into bed, she gasped involuntarily. Near her pillow lay a small packet which she had failed to notice before. She hesitated, then, with trembling fingers, she picked it up and unwrapped it slowly. Her eyes widened with surprise as the contents lay exposed in her hand—her silver watch!

For a stunned moment she stared at it in utter astonishment. Then her eyes turned back to the open window. It was the only means of access to her room; the door was still securely locked as were the other doors to her apartment. But . . . who had brought the packet? And why? She ran to the window and looked out again. But outside, all was still and deserted.

Could it be that that wretched man had actually had the nerve to come into her bedroom? She paled at the thought. Why, he could have murdered her in her bed had he so wished! She looked again at her watch, puzzled but nevertheless very pleased by its return.

What an odd incident, she thought, yawning and getting into bed again. But it was too late to think about it now. Perhaps some reasonable explanation would emerge in the morning . . .

In spite of the disturbed night she had spent, Melissa found herself wide awake with the first light. Quickly, she rose and ran to the window. All thoughts of her strange experience during the night vanished as her eyes fell upon the magnificent panorama before her. The sky was already beginning to change from pale pink to a light, eggshell blue dotted with fleecy white clouds.

The house stood high on the peak of a hill, its sides clothed in lush greenery. Beautiful flowering trees and shrubs speckled the garden, their blossoms hanging down in great clusters. At the bottom of the hill ran a slow, meandering stream. The ribbon of road went winding down the hill into the far distance, disappearing among the white, flat-roofed houses of Altabad town. The house was surrounded by gardens, all dreadfully overgrown and weeds covered most of the paved paths. But she could see that the estate must have once been beautiful indeed. This was the view her father must have gazed upon thousands of times from this very window.

Not willing to wait another moment, Melissa hastily washed and slipped into a light cotton dress. She ran down the marble staircase, through the main entrance, into the garden. Many years ago, her father had sent her a watercolour painted by himself, of the house. She ran down the garden to locate the exact spot from where the picture had been painted. Then she stopped and looked back, thrilled to be standing in the same place.

As she stared up at the imposing view, she remembered all the childish fantasies she had woven around the yellow house with the dark green shutters. Many were the daydreams in which she had floated, wraith-like, through its spacious rooms. She had imagined fabulous balls with soldiers in gay, red uniforms and ladies in shimmering Indian silks; she had heard the soft strains of waltzes and violins as she whirled around the elegant drawing room on the arm of some handsome officer. Sometimes, she recalled, her imagination had even evoked the fragrance of the colourful blossoms draped gracefully over the balustrades of the terrace above the portico . . .

In the bright light of day, she noticed that the yellow paint was peeling in many places, as was the green of the shutters. One window hung loose on its hinges and some of the glass panes were broken. A few bricks had come loose on the ledge of the roof and she could see gaps in the walls. There is a great deal to be done, she said to herself. But what my mountain of light needs more than anything else, is to be lived in and to be loved.

As she strolled round the house curiously, she saw a row of outhouses at the back where, she presumed, the servants lived with their families. Through the trees down below, she saw a glint of the river. Next to the servants' quarters were the stables and a large barn for a carriage, both empty. She would probably have to acquire a coach and horses. She decided to mention this to Mohan Das in due course.

Back in her rooms upstairs, Zarina was waiting with tea and breakfast of fresh melon and cereal.

'Madam sleep well?' Zarina asked smiling, laying the breakfast on a table in a corner of the terrace.

Melissa hesitated, wondering whether to mention the night's incident to Zarina, then decided not to. It would not do for the story to become common gossip in Altabad! She would have to think up some simple explanation to give Zarina about the return of her watch.

'Yes, Zarina,' she said, sitting down to eat, 'I slept very well indeed, thank you.'

'Excuse, Madam,' said Zarina, 'Hafiz here.'

'Who is Hafiz?'

'Hafiz work in garden.'

'Very well,' said Melissa, 'I would like to see him after breakfast. Please ask him to come up later.'

Judging by the size of the servants' quarters, there must be dozens of employees at Koh-i-noor. In a day or two, Melissa decided, she would ask Mohan Das to introduce them all to her so that she could get the household organised and allocate duties. She was determined not to spend more than absolutely necessary on running her home in spite of the generous amount the Maharaja had gifted her. Mr Winterton had already invested her capital wisely in England and she would have to satisfy all her requirements out of the interest monies he would send her from time to time.

Breakfast over, Zarina ushered in Hafiz. He was old and shrivelled and leaned heavily on a stick as he shuffled onto the terrace. Melissa smiled.

'I am very pleased to meet you, Hafiz. I learn that you work in the gardens?'

Hafiz said nothing. He merely stared at her through old, troubled eyes. When he finally spoke, his voice trembled with emotion.

'You go back England,' he said gruffly, 'Altabad no good.'

Melissa stared at him in astonishment. Then she laughed. 'I have only just arrived here, Hafiz. Why should I go back?'

The old man shook his head vigorously from side to side and repeated doggedly, 'You go home. Altabad *bad* place!'

Melissa felt a twinge of irritation. 'I have no intention of returning to England yet, Hafiz,' she said sharply, 'so we shall just have to drop the subject!'

'They kill Guy *sahib*,' the old gardener said fearfully, 'now they also kill you, Missy.'

It was such a totally unexpected remark that, for a moment, Melissa felt herself go quite cold. 'What . . . what did you say?' she asked, bewildered.

'I work for Guy *sahib*. I *love* Guy *sahib*!' The old man's eyes filled with tears. 'They not let you live in house, Missy. This *bad* house!'

Melissa's heart contracted at the use of the special name her father had given her, but she had no idea what the old man was talking about. Perhaps he was rambling?

Very gently she said, 'This house was my father's home, Hafiz. My father loved this house and he wanted me to share it with him. You must help me to make the gardens beautiful again.'

'I frightened for you, Missy,' the gardener persisted. 'They kill you too!'

'What nonsense!' exclaimed Melissa lightly. 'No one is going to kill me! Why should they? I know not a soul in Altabad yet.' Gently but firmly, she propelled him towards the door. Really, she thought in exasperation, what next?

As soon as Hafiz left, Melissa decided the first thing she must do is to make a tour of the house. Its two storeys contained so many rooms and balconies that she felt she would never learn her way around without an initial guided tour. But, just as she was going to call for Mohan Das, she heard horses' hoofs and the sound of carriage wheels rumbling up the drive. Now, I wonder who that can be, she asked herself curiously. Peering over the terrace wall, Zarina said, 'Madam have visitor.'

'Visitor?' Melissa asked, surprised.

'Madam Dr Herbert, she come.'

Anne Morrison had mentioned Celia Herbert to Melissa and she felt pleasantly nervous at the thought of entertaining her first caller in Altabad. She immediately asked Zarina to bring her upstairs into the drawing room.

Celia Herbert, small and round with a bright, cheerful face and untidy salt and pepper hair, bustled into the room a few moments later.

'My dear Miss Castlewood,' she said breathlessly, plumping herself down on the divan, 'I am so sorry to barge in like this as I know you only arrived last night and must have a thousand matters to attend to this morning. But the truth is,' she puffed a little trying to regain her breath, 'we are all *dying* to know what you are like and I just could not wait!'

Melissa laughed, instantly charmed by Celia Herbert's cheerful frankness. 'As you can see, Mrs Herbert, I am just a very ordinary English girl, rather confused and at a loss at the moment.'

Celia Herbert examined her critically, then shook her head very firmly. 'One thing I can tell you you are not, my dear,' she said, 'is *ordinary*. Why, my dear, you are *lovely*!'

Melissa coloured at the unexpected compliment and quickly changed the subject. 'I am so happy that you decided to call, Mrs Herbert. Anne Morrison and her husband John told me so much about you and your family.'

'Ah yes, we heard the Morrisons were bringing you out. Now, under no circumstances,' she added severely, 'must you feel lost. My dear, we are all here to help you. I am certain you and my daughter Stephanie will be great friends. She is just a mite younger than you.'

Melissa was touched. 'Thank you,' she said, 'I look forward to meeting your daughter and Dr Herbert.'

'Well now, that is really what I called about. Dr Herbert and I are having a small supper party tomorrow evening. Most of the English people in Altabad will be there and we would be so delighted if you could come too. Do say you will!'

'Why,' exclaimed Melissa, pleased, 'I would like to, very much. How kind of you to ask me.'

'Nonsense!' said Mrs Herbert, rising, 'It's wonderful for us to at last have some fresh young English blood in Altabad and I daresay you will find yourself in great demand all round. I will send the carriage for you at seven, if that is not too early.'

'That would suit me very well,' said Melissa, 'thank you.'

'We are not a very exciting or young crowd,' Celia Herbert said apologetically on the way down, 'but we do have our bright spots, like Maree Chandler, although, of course, some say . . .' she broke off hastily and blew her nose. 'And, of course, Gareth may be there, Gareth Caldwell. He promised to come but, then, you know Gareth!'

'As a matter of fact,' reminded Melissa gently, 'I do not.'

'Of course not!' exclaimed Mrs Herbert, 'how foolish of me! But then, you will.' She climbed into her carriage heavily and asked through the window. 'Are you planning to stay with us for a while?'

'Yes,' said Melissa very positively, 'I am planning to stay for a while.'

'Oh, good,' said Mrs Herbert heartily waving her handkerchief in the air, 'I *am* pleased. We could certainly do with a pretty young face in Altabad. Until tomorrow then, *au revoir*.'

Melissa waved back and slowly walked up the stairs to her rooms, smiling. She had no doubt she was going to like the rest of the Herbert family. There was something very reassuring about Celia Herbert with her homely, English face and down-to-earth manner.

Getting back now to her interrupted business, Melissa sent for Mohan Das.

'Madam wishes to inspect the rooms?' he asked courteously. 'It will be my pleasure to escort Madam around personally.' He suggested they start from the top floor and work their way down.

The house had many rooms on both its floors, some large, some small, but all with lofty ceilings and cool marble floors. A few were furnished with sad-looking dust covers on the furniture. Others were bare. I shall have to get all these rooms aired and cleaned, thought Melissa to herself.

Aloud she said, 'I think we should start by having the house painted, don't you think so?'

There was a pause, then Mohan Das asked, 'Madam is planning to stay for some time, then?' His voice remained passive but Melissa felt a sudden tension in the air.

'Yes, of course,' she said firmly, 'I do plan to stay for *quite* some time.'

'I see.' His manner, cold and formal, seemed to become even more so. Now, *he* wants me to go away as well, thought Melissa curiously. I wonder why?

They were on the ground-floor verandah at the back of the house when they passed by the entrance of a dark corridor that led inwards.

'What is down there?' Melissa asked.

'This section of the house was badly damaged during an earthquake,' Mohan Das explained. 'As Madam can see, the ceiling has to be propped up with bamboo poles. It is unsafe to go down there as the slightest disturbance may bring down the ceiling.'

The end of the corridor was lost in gloom. Large chunks of plaster lay in untidy heaps on the floor. The walls were covered with thick, black cobwebs.

'Ugh!' shuddered Melissa, 'I do not think I would like to venture inside!'

They went down to the riverside through a thicket. The water was cool and green and dappled with sunshine.

'How very pretty!' Melissa exclaimed, charmed by the scene. 'I shall come down with my pastels one day, and make a picture of this to send to my friends in England.'

She sensed, rather than saw, Mohan Das stiffen. 'It is not advisable,' he said coldly, 'The river is full of crocodiles that often come up on the banks.'

'Oh, I shall be very careful,' said Melissa nettled by his tone. 'And if I do see a crocodile, so much the better. It will make a more exciting picture!'

Mohan Das said nothing but she could see that he was not pleased. He bowed formally. 'If Madam has no further duties for me, I would like to visit my sick mother in the town.'

'I am sorry to hear that your mother is not well,' said Melissa, 'Yes, certainly you may go.'

Without another word, he clicked his heels and left. Melissa stared after him for a moment. There is something about this man, she thought uneasily, that I do not trust!

The rest of the day went in unpacking her trunks, cleaning out the cupboards and arranging her possessions. After tea she sat down to write letters to the Morrisons and to friends in England. She filled page after page, writing very fast, her hand trying to keep pace with her thoughts. There was so much news to give!

By the time she had completed her letters, eaten a light supper and washed and changed, it was nearing eleven o'clock. She felt tired, but pleasantly so. I think I shall sleep very well tonight, she thought, as she lay down in bed and Zarina extinguished the lamp.

But, in spite of her tiredness, sleep would not come. Her mind seemed strangely ill at ease, disturbing thoughts chasing one another unceasingly. All her unease seemed to centre around Hafiz's very strange remark this morning—*they kill Guy* sahib. What on earth did he mean? Was the old man senile, or . . . the alternative was too horrible to contemplate. She *knew* her father had died of cholera! *They kill you too, Missy . . . that*, of course, was too absurd to even consider! Resolutely, she put the entire conversation out of her mind, deciding that Hafiz had, indeed, been rambling. It was the only explanation possible.

But even then, sleep continued to elude her. With a sigh, she finally rose and stood by the window. The moon was high in the heavens and the garden was bathed in bright silver. She decided to take a stroll in the open to clear her mind of its restlessness. She slipped on a light robe over her nightdress and, lantern in hand, went quietly down the stairs.

It was a lovely night and there was nobody about. All was quiet. Soon, as she strolled up and down the garden paths, she felt herself calm down. She took a few final breaths, marvelling again at the exotic perfumes of an Indian night, then started back towards the house.

As she was turning the corner at the back, she suddenly heard the faint but frantic mewing of a cat. Melissa stood still for a while and listened. Yes, there it was again. Poor thing, she thought, it is in trouble. Maybe it is stuck somewhere or injured. She retraced her steps and, as she did so, the mewing became steadily louder. Working out her bearings, she came to the point from which she could hear it at its loudest. She looked up—and stopped. Before her was the opening to the damaged corridor! Oh dear, she thought in dismay. It is down there, somewhere. The mewing was becoming more and more anguished. She was sure the poor creature was badly hurt. She looked around to see if anybody was around to help, but the compound was deserted.

Drawing her robe closer around her and gritting her teeth, Melissa stepped gingerly into the rubble-strewn corridor. She took care to tread very softly for fear of disturbing the bamboo poles that supported the weak ceiling. The dreadful cobwebs looked even larger in the flickering light of the lantern. As she turned the corner at the end of the corridor, the mewing became very loud indeed. Melissa looked around, then stopped dead in surprise. The mewing came from *underneath* the floor!

Wonderingly, she placed the lantern on the ground and pushed the rubble aside with her feet. As the floor cleared, she noticed that one flagstone had an iron ring set in it. She bent down and listened. The cat was directly beneath the flagstone!

Melissa touched the iron ring nervously and gave it a tug. The stone did not budge. She turned it a little to one side—and fell back with a muffled scream. The flagstone had flown open smoothly and silently as if on oiled wheels! At the same instant, a big black ball of fur flung itself against her legs, then flew down the corridor mewing loudly.

Melissa stared at the square opening at her feet, her

heart thudding wildly, her hands cold. She stood
frozen for a moment, listening. But there was no
sound from anywhere except the cries of the rescued
cat now safe in the garden. Pulling herself together,
she lifted the lantern and peered down the hole. It
contained a flight of stone steps leading down into a
basement. Carefully, lantern in hand, she tried the
first step, then the second. They seemed to be quite
firm. Slowly, she climbed down and found herself in a
medium-sized basement room. The room was empty
of human presence—but there was plenty of evidence
of human occupation! Along one wall were lined
some string cots such as used by the poor people in
India. On each cot was a bedroll. There were signs of
a makeshift kitchen with saucepans and dishes and a
paraffin stove.

Melissa stared at the sight before her eyes in growing amazement. What on earth was all this? A servants' room? But she knew all the servants lived in the
outhouses. How very odd!

On the other side of the basement room was a door
fitted into an alcove. Very quietly, Melissa tiptoed up
to it and put her ear against the wooden panels. She
could hear nothing. With her heart beating loudly
against her ribs, but unable to contain her consuming
curiosity, she swallowed hard and pushed outwards.
The door opened immediately and without a sound.

She gasped. What faced her was a room very different to the one she had just left. It was small and neat
and well appointed. In fact, it looked very much like
an English office! The walls were covered with maps
and charts. A desk with green baize top stood against
one wall and was stacked with folders and files next to

writing paper, pen holders and inkpots. On the table
stood a shining brass lamp burning now with a low
flame. Three English briar pipes and a pouch of
tobacco lay in a small wooden bowl. The room also
had a canvas camp cot draped with a green bedcover
and a small cupboard with brass handles. In an alcove,
half covered by a curtain, stood a wash stand with
clean towels hanging on a nearby rail.

Melissa observed the room, stunned. Who did it
belong to? And why? In the opposite wall she suddenly noticed another door. She tiptoed up to it, hardly
daring to breathe, and listened. There was utter
silence. Taking a deep breath, she pushed the door
outwards. Again, the door swung back soundlessly
and before her, in the pale light of her lantern, lay a
long, narrow tunnel, its sides curved and overhung
with mildew glistening with water. The far end of the
tunnel was lost in silent gloom. A tunnel going *under*
the river—she could see that the floor of the passage-
way sloped downwards continuously.

She stood transfixed with shock. I have stumbled on
to something I am not supposed to know about, she
thought, and was gripped with fear. Who occupied
these rooms and for what purpose? Should she dare
venture further? But the question was answered for
her suddenly and without warning.

In the far, black distance of the downward tunnel,
she saw the beginnings of an uncertain light. Faint
echoes of human voices reverberated against the
stones, sounding strangely hollow.

With a horrified gasp, Melissa closed the door and,
lifting her robe with one hand, ran nimbly back into
the basement room and then up the flight of stone

steps. I must not be caught in here, she told herself frantically. She pushed hard at the flagstone above her head. It refused to budge! Oh my God, she almost sobbed in desperation, I am going to be discovered!

She ran back into the smaller room, her breath exploding in short, painful gasps. The voices were louder and she could also hear the echo of heavy footsteps on the tunnel floor. Looking around frantically for a hiding place, she ran to the alcove containing the wash stand. Quickly pulling the curtain over, she made herself into a small, tight ball and crouched down in the far corner behind the stand. She extinguished the lantern and, in the gloom, breathed a silent prayer.

Not a moment too soon! Suddenly the room was flooded with light and sounds of heavy movement. She listened fearfully. As far as she could make out, there were two men in the room. They were talking loudly and easily, but in Hindustani. She strained her ears to see if she could pick up a few words of possible English—and suddenly she did. Her own name! Melissa stuffed her handkerchief into her mouth to stop herself from screaming. They were talking about her!

She listened again, carefully, certain that any minute they would hear the cacophonous thumping of her heart. Even though they still spoke in Hindustani, she suddenly felt there was something vaguely familiar about one of the voices. She listened again carefully and then it came to her in a flash. Mohan Das! One of the voices belonged to him. But—what was he doing here? Had he not gone to Altabad to visit his sick mother? And who was the other man? The voice was deep and very masculine and it had a strange intonation to it. Before she could puzzle it out, the voice broke into a laugh and then, unexpectedly, into English!

'She is going to be a damned nuisance, I can tell you that!' it said. 'But never mind. We will think of a way to get rid of her. You had better take the diamonds over immediately. They will be waiting for them. Not a bad haul, eh?' The voice laughed again and Melissa realised why it had sounded strange in Hindustani. It belonged to an Englishman!

'Very good, sir,' Mohan Das replied. 'I shall be back within half an hour with the message.' There was a sound of receding footsteps and then silence.

Who was the Englishman in the room? Terrified, but unable to control her raging curiosity, Melissa inched her way forward to peer through a chink in the curtain. The man was sitting at the desk with his back—wide-shouldered and muscular—towards her, writing furiously. He paused to fill and light a pipe. As he turned in profile, she saw that his features were sharp and aquiline and indeed European. His movements, as he puffed at the pipe, were slow and relaxed. He seemed completely at home! What if he lives here, thought Melissa in panic. How will I ever get away?

Suddenly, to her horror, she felt her nose twitch dangerously as the dust in the alcove climbed up her nostrils. Oh my God, she thought, I am going to sneeze! She crushed her handkerchief against her nose, her hands trembling with fear. Oh sweet God, please, *please* do not let me sneeze . . .

'A-*TISH*-OO!'

In the confined space of the alcove, the sneeze sounded like an explosion!

With a startled oath, the figure of the man sprang up, sending the chair crashing to the floor. The curtain was pulled aside roughly and she found herself staring, petrified, into the furious, contorted face of the Englishman—and the barrel of a gun!

For a split second they stared at each other, one in terror, the other in black fury.

'Who the devil are you—and what the hell are you doing down here?' The Englishman spoke through clenched teeth, his voice soft but like steel, the gun not wavering for a moment.

Realising that the game was indeed up and she might as well make the best of a desperate situation, Melissa rose to her feet shakily and pulled herself up with as much dignity as she could muster under the circumstances. As the light fell on her face, a look of utter astonishment replaced the anger in the Englishman's expression.

'I might well ask you the same question,' Melissa retorted icily, trying hard to control the tremor in her voice, 'considering that you are on my property.'

The Englishman, who appeared to be in his late 'twenties, was tall, well-built with thick, unruly hair and piercing light hazel eyes. His body, taut and rugged, gave the impression of litheness—and power. Melissa, however, noticed none of this as she faced him haughtily, trying to suppress the humiliation of having been caught in so undignified a situation.

The young man seemed taken aback by her question. Then, astonishingly, he threw back his head and laughed.

'*Touché!*' he exclaimed, putting the gun back in its holster at his waist and bowing in mock fashion. He tilted his head to one side and subjected her to an insolent, amused look. Melissa felt herself redden.

'Melissa Castlewood,' he said slowly, 'So, we meet at last, albeit in rather unconventional circumstances.'

'You know who I am?' she asked, surprised.

'Well, you said you were the lady of the manor, so I presume you must be Miss Castlewood.'

His tone of insolence irritated her further. 'And who, pray,' she asked cuttingly, 'are *you*?'

He bowed again, this time even lower. 'I do beg your pardon. My astonishment at finding you here snuggled against my wash stand, seems to have got the better of my manners. Gareth Caldwell at your service.'

Melissa could not repress a sudden start. So, *this* was the arrogant Gareth Caldwell—the man no two people seemed to agree upon!

'You still have not answered my second question,' she reminded him with asperity, regaining her composure. 'What are you doing in my house without either my knowledge or my permission?'

Caldwell seemed at a loss for a moment but Melissa could see that, beneath his nonchalance, his mind was working furiously. He suddenly shook his head as if in disgust.

'Damned women!' he exploded, throwing his hands up. 'Trust them to snoop around where they have no business!' Then, noticing that she still stood inside the alcove, he pulled the entire curtain to one side. 'I suppose you had better come out of there now. You seem to have done a good night's work!'

'So have you,' flung back Melissa, infuriated by his offensive tone. Picking up her lantern, she stepped into the room.

'Thank goodness you don't understand Hindustani yet,' he said angrily. 'How the dickens did you get down here?'

'Through your clever trap door! And I was *not* snooping around, as you put it. In case you have forgotten, this happens to be *my* property and I have a right to know what you are doing here.'

Caldwell turned away, straightened the chair and offered it to her. Melissa shook her head impatiently. 'I would just like my question answered please! I have no intention of staying a moment longer than necessary.'

He shrugged, picked up his pipe and, very deliberately, began to puff on it, ignoring her completely. Melissa looked at him in exasperation.

'Do not try and evade my question,' she said, 'I demand an answer!'

'What I am doing here,' said Gareth Caldwell lightly and very casually, 'is, I regret to say, none of your business.'

'*Oh!*' Melissa was almost speechless at the man's incredible effrontery. Her face went white. 'How *dare* you insult me in my own home,' she raged, 'How *dare* you . . . !'

He remained unperturbed by her outburst but suddenly he seemed to relax. 'All right,' he said, 'since you insist on an answer, you might as well sit down while I give it to you.'

'I do not *wish* to sit down!'

He shrugged again. 'As you like. In that case, *I* will sit down. I've had a damned hard day.' Calmly, he proceeded to make himself comfortable in the chair, swinging his legs on to the desk, perfectly at ease. He opened a drawer and took out an apple. 'Would you care for one?' he asked politely as if offering a sandwich at a tea party.

'No, I would *not*!' Melissa said, outraged. 'I am still waiting for an explanation.'

But Gareth Caldwell seemed in no hurry to give her one. He unhooked a penknife from his belt and carefully started to peel the apple, giving it his full concentration. Melissa could do nothing but stand and watch helplessly, aware that the interview was not being conducted to her advantage. The man was impossibly arrogant. John Morrison was absolutely right about him!

Melissa stood fuming while he continued to ignore her, totally immersed in his enjoyment of the wretched apple. Her angry eyes strayed round the room again. What were all those maps for, she wondered. And the folders? Her eyes focused on the cupboard and on the floor in front of it. Almost at her feet lay one black glove, as if dropped in a hurry when its pair was thrust hastily into the cupboard. Melissa frowned for a brief moment—then the blood in her veins seemed to turn to ice. Before her eyes floated the vision of a black finger at the end of which dangled her silver watch!

Very slowly, as if glazed, her eyes went back to the man at the desk. For the first time she noticed that he was dressed entirely in black! With a strangled gasp, she clutched her throat with a shaking hand.

Gareth Caldwell turned quickly and, noticing the pallor of her face, jumped to his feet.

'Let me fetch you a glass of water,' he said, 'You certainly look as if you need it. But, for goodness' sakes, don't faint down here, or it will be a devil of a job carrying you up those damned steps!'

Melissa took the glass of water he held out, with a trembling hand. She drank thirstily, her eyes stealing back in disbelief to the object on the floor. Caldwell followed her gaze—and went rigid.

'Damn!' she heard him curse under his breath. '*Damn!*'

How could it be she thought wildly? The idea was absolutely absurd! Yet, before her was the evidence of her own eyes. Senseless as it seemed, it appeared to be the only explanation possible!

'You,' she whispered finally in a voice barely audible. '*You* are Sher Singh?'

Caldwell's eyes narrowed. His face became very still—and deadly. His whole body seemed to tauten like a coiled spring. Then, just as rapidly, the tall, lithe figure loosened. His face became quite calm.

'Yes,' he said, almost casually. 'I am Sher Singh.'

CHAPTER
THREE

MELISSA continued to stare at Gareth Caldwell, her eyes wide with shock.

'You, an *Englishman*, are Sher Singh?' she asked incredulously, 'a common thief and outlaw?'

'Thief and outlaw, yes,' said Caldwell cheerfully, 'but common? Never! As no doubt everyone had already told you, I am a most *un*common thief. By the way, you did get your watch back, I trust?'

'Yes,' said Melissa with stiff formality, still outraged at the disclosure he had made, 'I . . . I must thank you, I suppose but . . . I must also ask you not to . . . to make it a habit to enter my bedroom at will.'

'In that case,' he said mildly, 'you must not make it a habit to sleep with your window open. You never know *who* might walk in.'

Melissa flushed. 'I have no doubt you are merely trying to gain time to fabricate some tale to me.'

'Actually, yes,' he grinned. 'I am wondering just how much it is safe to tell you. I have never yet known a woman who could keep her mouth shut—and I doubt if you are an exception. Would you like an orange? I seem to have missed my dinner and am devilishly hungry.'

Melissa shook her head grimly. Really! This man was the utter limit!

'You are a wanted bandit,' she said, 'and whatever story you choose to concoct for me, I intend to do my duty as I see fit. I have no desire to be accused of harbouring a murderer.'

'I have never murdered anyone in my life,' he said placidly, 'although, I must admit, on occasion the temptation is very strong. Like now.'

'*Oh!*' Melissa stared at him in horror.

'But I won't give in to it,' he said quickly. 'At least not tonight.' He was mocking her openly and Melissa was furious. 'However,' he continued, 'since I do happen to be an uninvited guest on your premises, perhaps a small explanation is called for. You might as well sit down.'

Melissa sank slowly into the chair, much too shaken to protest any more. 'I shall not believe one single word of what you say,' she said faintly.

Caldwell raised his eyebrows. 'That,' he said carelessly, 'is your privilege. Frankly, it hardly matters a hoot what you do choose to believe! But if you "do your duty", as you so piously put it, you may end up making a fool of yourself.'

Suddenly, his bantering tone changed and he turned to face her squarely, his strange, tawny eyes in dead earnest.

'Why have you come to Altabad?' he asked abruptly, almost angrily.

Melissa was taken aback by the intensity of his tone. 'I have come to Altabad because . . . I chose to,' she retorted with asperity, 'Not that it is the slightest concern of yours.'

'Unfortunately, my dear, upright, duty-bound Miss Castlewood, it is of the utmost concern to me.' He began pacing up and down the small room like a caged tiger. 'Your life here is unsafe. Return to England where you will be away from harm.'

'Harm?' cried Melissa, 'Why should anyone wish to harm me?'

'Because,' said Caldwell slowly with cold emphasis on every word, 'you are your father's daughter and because Koh-i-noor now belongs to you.'

She shook her head in bewilderment. 'What has my father to do with all this?'

'Your father was killed for the same reason that you will be.'

Melissa went white with shock. 'My father died of cholera,' she whispered.

Caldwell stopped abruptly in his tracks, his face stunned. 'Oh my God,' he breathed, 'You didn't know?'

Dumbly, Melissa shook her head, her eyes filling with tears.

For a moment Caldwell said nothing, struggling with words, his face a picture of remorse. When he spoke, his voice was unexpectedly gentle. 'I am deeply sorry in that case, to have thrust the information on you with unthinking brutality.' He turned away quickly to give her time to gather herself together again. For a while neither spoke. By the time he faced her again, she her regained her composure, only the pallor of her skin giving any indication of her feelings.

Very quietly she said, 'No. I did not know. Please tell me what happened.'

Caldwell sat down on the camp cot. 'Your father was . . . found dead in his bed one morning, not at Koh-i-noor,' he added hastily seeing her expression of horror, 'but while out camping in the jungle. He had been poisoned.'

'Who by?' asked Melissa, her voice barely audible.

Caldwell paused. 'There were suspicions but nothing was ever proved and nobody was apprehended. Not wishing to make the tragedy public, the authorities here decided to hush up the matter. It was declared that Colonel Castlewood had succumbed to cholera. Which does not mean that no investigations were made. Indeed, the British Resident at the time made every effort to find the assassin. As I said, there were . . . suspicions, but no proof.'

'So, a crime as heinous as this has gone unpunished?' Melissa asked, her heart wrenched with pain.

'But,' said Caldwell quietly, 'it will not. That much I can assure you of.'

Melissa stared at him blankly. 'How . . . how do *you* know all this?'

For a moment Caldwell was nonplussed. Then, he took refuge in the act of emptying, refilling and relighting his pipe, giving himself time to think. When he answered her question, his manner had again changed to one of casual nonchalance.

'Oh, I have ways and means of gathering information. After all, in a profession such as mine, I have to!'

'You mean . . . the profession of a bandit!'

'Certainly! We bandits have to live too, you know.'

Melissa was appalled at his flippancy. 'You feel no sense of shame, no . . . no pangs of conscience at disgracing the flag of your country?' Melissa felt her temper rise again.

'None at all,' Caldwell said cheerfully, 'The British

flag has many other heroes to do it honour. The sun of the Empire shines quite successfully without my help.'

'In that case,' said Melissa spiritedly, disgusted with his outrageous attitude, 'I see my duty quite clearly. I shall *not* permit you to abuse *my* home as a hideout for your nefarious activities!'

Caldwell's voice became again like chilled steel. 'I must warn you not to reveal to anyone what you have seen and heard tonight—or you may not even live to regret it!'

Melissa's throat went dry at the menace contained in his words. 'You would kill me?' she whispered fearfully.

'No. But somebody else would.'

'*Why?*' cried Melissa in frustrated rage.

Caldwell rose from the cot abruptly and opened the door leading into the large basement room. 'I can tell you no more,' he said shortly. A dozen questions leaped to Melissa's lips but Gareth Caldwell stopped her with an impatient gesture. 'Mohan Das should be returning any moment and there will be hell to pay if he finds you here.'

'Who *is* Mohan Das?'

'You do not need to know who he is or why he is here. It is enough for you to know that he is at Koh-i-noor to ensure your safety. Trust him.'

He picked up her lantern and relit it for her, then stood pointedly beside the open door. He is dismissing me as if I were one of his . . . his *gang*, thought Melissa angrily. Grabbing the lantern he held out to her, she flounced past him and walked up to the flight of stone steps that led to the trap door.

'Neither of you need concern yourselves with me,' she said tightly, 'or with my safety. I am old enough to look after myself!'

'I concern myself with you for only one reason, make no mistake about that. It is because . . .' he stopped, then threw his hands up. 'It does not matter at the moment.'

'Because,' said Melissa acidly, 'you have made my house into a very cosy hideout for yourself! No wonder I am "a damned nuisance", as you yourself put it so charmingly some time ago, whom you would greatly love to "get rid of". Is that not why you want me to return to England, so that you can carry on your criminal activities in peace? I do not believe a word of the cock and bull stories you have concocted for my benefit!'

Gareth Caldwell shrugged again and smiled blandly. 'If that is what you choose to believe. And now, I must ask you to go or Mohan Das will be most annoyed.' He pressed a small button on the underside of the flagstone—which she had not noticed—and the stone slid back smoothly. Then, he stood aside to let her pass.

In spite of her brave words of defiance, Melissa felt the icy fingers of fear in her heart. Her expression of bravado crumbled and her lips trembled. Very slowly, she began to climb the steps. As she passed by him, she paused. Without realising it, her face became that of a small, helpless child. He was standing very close; she could feel his breath on her face.

Very suddenly and almost imperceptibly, his hands rose and cupped her face. He bent his head down fleetingly and kissed her on the lips. It was an action of such delicacy, so much tenderness, that for a split second Melissa was hardly aware of what had happened. Then, as the colour rushed to her face, her hands began to tremble so that she almost dropped her lantern.

He lowered his hands immediately. 'Never come down here again,' he said softly. 'You have no idea how much depends upon your discretion. All I can say is—everything is not as it seems. Goodnight.'

Without being aware of exactly how, she found herself standing all by herself in the deserted, derelict corridor. The flagstone at her feet was once again back in place. She was alone.

For a moment, Melissa stood rooted to the spot, the colour in her face still high, the lantern shaking in her hand uncontrollably. She put her other hand up to her lips, lost in confused thought. His kiss, as light as a moonbeam's touch, was still warm on her mouth. Quite involuntarily, she shivered as her body tingled with unfamiliar excitement, limp with a hitherto unknown pleasure.

Then, she took a deep breath, resolutely throwing off the strange sensations that seemed to course through her limbs. She looked around and listened, but the night was silent. Slowly, she threaded her way out of the corridor and made her way back to her room.

The morning sun was streaming in through her window when Melissa finally awakened from her sleep. Even though it was late, she lay still in bed for a while, allowing her thoughts to pour over her lazily. In the light of bright day, the previous night's events seemed

strange and bizarre, almost like a particularly vivid
dream. Could it all have been a dream? Yet, she knew
that it was all only too real. Last night Gareth Caldwell's unexpected kiss had sent her senses reeling, but
this morning the extraordinary things he had told her
stood out in sharp relief. Her darling Papa had been
murdered; Hafiz had been right! Or . . . had he?
Could she believe what Gareth Caldwell had told her?
What value could she put on the word of a self-
confessed criminal, a man who respected neither
Queen nor country? And yet . . . there had been
something in his manner that inspired confidence.
Was he just a clever rogue with a glib tongue—or a
ruthless usurper of other mens' property?

Her deliberations left her even more confused than
before. Added to that was the pain of knowing how
her Papa had died, not peacefully and naturally at the
will of God—but brutally and callously, at the hands
of an assassin. It was a distressing revelation indeed,
made bearable only by the distance in time.

The delicious mint-flavoured tea that Zarina
brought in to her did much to soothe the disturbances
in her mind. I must stop brooding, she told herself
sadly. What has happened has happened; I cannot
bring Papa back by neglecting my duties.

Firmly, and with a determined effort, she shook off
her depression and, after a light breakfast of cool
melon and cereal, she went down into the garden in
search of Hafiz. She was sorely tempted to question
him more, but decided not to. It would be useless
distressing the old man with questions he might not be
able to answer.

The rest of the morning passed off pleasantly.

Together with Hafiz, she toured from one end of the gardens to the other, planning and considering how best to bring them back to vibrant life. Hafiz was now too old for manual work but his two sons, he informed Melissa, would perform the strenuous tasks under his supervision.

Then, nervously, she sent for Mohan Das, wondering if Gareth Caldwell had informed him of her visit last night. But Mohan Das, when he arrived a few minutes later, remained impassive, his face betraying nothing.

'How is your mother now?' Melissa asked.

'She is well, thank you. But I could not return until the morning.'

Melissa knew he was lying, but said nothing. *Trust him*, Caldwell had said. She was not even sure of Gareth Caldwell—how could she be sure of Mohan Das? Oh, she thought in exasperation, it is all so confusing. I must not give in to idle introspection again. Resolutely, she decided to put last night out of her mind—for the moment anyway. Accompanied by Mohan Das, she set about examining Koh-i-noor's many store rooms and organising the various duties of her staff.

Later, when she went back upstairs for lunch, she sat on the terrace and looked down upon the grounds of Koh-i-noor where Hafiz and his two sons were already busy putting her instructions into practice. Watching them at work, she felt her spirits rise. Breathing in the rich fragrances of a summer afternoon and listening to the gentle hum of bees as they engaged in collection of honey for the hives at the bottom of the garden, she began to feel a sense of peace come over her. This is my home, she thought. I belong to this place and it belongs to me. If Gareth Caldwell was under the impression that he could 'get rid of her'—for whatever reason!—he was sadly mistaken. No one was going to deprive her of what was rightfully hers!

It was much later, after she had had her afternoon siesta, that she suddenly remembered, with a guilty start, that today was the day of the Herberts' supper party. The events of the previous night had driven all thought of it from her mind. Hurriedly, she went to her almirah to examine her clothes and to decide what would be appropriate wear for the evening. She felt elated and nervous at the same time at the prospect of meeting so many new people at once. It was so long since she had been to a party!

After some deliberation, Melissa settled on a dress of eggshell blue satin with a high bodice and a delicate spray of embroidered bluebells down the front. Forced by Mrs Rutherford, she had embarked on a shopping spree in London before she had sailed. 'You will meet many elegant people in India,' Mrs Rutherford had argued, 'You must be well dressed now that you can afford to be so.' She remembered how guilty she had felt when the bill for her purchases had added up to more than she had earned in a year in Cornhill! Nevertheless, she had been thrilled at becoming the owner of a wardrobe so exquisite and so extensive. She had had so little in her life, having always been of necessity satisfied with a series of hand-me-downs.

When she was dressed, she surveyed herself in the full-length mirror in her dressing room. Would she be over-dressed, she wondered? Under-dressed? Did women wear gloves in India as they did in England? Oh dear, she thought, I should have remembered to ask Anne for some advice. India was so different to England in every way. Nevertheless, she decided, she would certainly pass muster. She brushed her hair until it shone like polished copper, and tied it in a simple Grecian knot into which Zarina placed a lovely white flower. Her face, pretty and smooth skinned, needed no cosmetic help. Her wide-set eyes, large and fringed with thick lashes, sparkled naturally with suppressed excitement and her youth and innocence gave a golden glow to a naturally perfect complexion. Her lips, now parted in a slight smile, were the colour of pale peaches, soft and luscious. Observing herself in the mirror with Zarina gazing at her in rapt admiration, Melissa found herself wondering if Gareth Caldwell would be at the party, as he had promised Mrs Herbert. The thought brought a quick flush of pink to her cheeks and her breath quickened, much to her annoyance. She put her nose up in the air. Gareth Caldwell was an arrogant, insolent young *pup*, she decided, recalling the words of John Morrison. He had no right to expect her reticence about his disgraceful, shameful secret. She would most certainly have to inform the authorities, but . . . why did she feel reluctant to do so? It was very annoying!

It was almost seven-thirty p.m. by the time Melissa arrived at the Herberts', the carriage having arrived exactly at seven.

'My dear Melissa—I may call you Melissa, may I not?—you do look utterly ravishing!' exclaimed Celia Herbert clasping her hands warmly as soon as she arrived at the neat little bungalow where the Herberts lived near the Altabad hospital. 'What a charming dress! I am afraid, we tend to be a little behind the times with London fashions. They take so long to arrive. Come, my dear, everyone is waiting to meet you.'

An expectant hush descended upon the drawing room as Melissa entered. There were about a dozen people in the room and Melissa flushed as she felt everyone's eyes focus on her immediately. I must not appear awkward, she admonished herself nervously, I must behave with perfect poise.

She immediately liked Dr George Herbert, short, plump and as cheerfully untidy as his wife. His eyes held a permanent twinkle and his shock of white hair trembled like a blancmange every time he laughed, which was often.

'What a pleasure it is to have you here in Altabad, my dear Melissa,' he said without formality, 'You must meet our daughter, Stephanie, who could do with some tutoring in how to dress like a real English lady.' Standing next to her father, plump and plain with a round, placid face, Stephanie laughed, not in the least put out by her father's remark. 'Not that it will make any difference to my appearance! Do come, Melissa. Everyone wants to be introduced.'

Stephanie handed her a glass of sparkling sherbet, then took charge of her firmly. The tall, official looking gentleman with imposing side whiskers, was Mr Fred Carstairs, the British Resident.

'I knew your late father, my dear,' he said, 'He was a very fine gentleman and a brave soldier.'

Melissa paused, wanting to ask so many questions but before she could decide on their formulation,

Stephanie whisked her away to meet somebody else. There were Tom and Milly Patterson (he was the Chief of Police), Gordon Hattersley who was something to do with the waterworks, Nigel Bannister, a young lieutenant in the British Army on leave from Fort St George and Roy Chandler, who, she knew, was in charge of the diamond mines.

'I should so love to visit your mines someday,' said Melissa. 'My father talked of them a great deal when I was a child.'

'Alas,' said Mr Chandler regretfully, 'the mines are in a high security area where civilians are not allowed. But I shall see if Mr Carstairs can be prevailed upon to issue you a permit.'

By the time she had met everyone, her head was spinning with names. In spite of determining not to do so, Melissa felt her eyes rove the room in search of Gareth Caldwell. He was nowhere to be seen. At the end of the large room, leaning gracefully on a grand piano, with one white gloved hand delicately holding a wine glass, stood the most strikingly beautiful woman Melissa had ever seen. She was very tall and slender, yet with an incredibly perfect, full figure which was encased in a shimmering taffeta gown of lime green—almost the same colour as her eyes. Her skin was like ivory satin, her high cheekbones tinged faintly with a becoming touch of red. Her hair, jet black and glossy, was piled high on her head, making her even taller, and pinned to one side of her head was a diamond brooch. She was, indeed, a beautiful woman—and was only too well aware of it.

'This,' said Stephanie, 'is Mrs Maree Chandler.'

Maree Chandler stretched out a long, languid hand

towards Melissa, smiling through half-parted lips and observing Melissa very closely, up and down.

'Ah,' she said softly, her voice low and husky, 'So, this is our long-awaited heiress, is it? They said you were like a perfect English rose and, of course, you are!' She made the comment sound like a sneer. Melissa felt herself flush.

'I am pleased to meet you, Mrs Chandler,' she replied coolly.

'And how do you like being mistress of Koh-i-noor?' Mrs Chandler persisted. 'Very different, I should imagine, to being—what was it you were in England? A companion?'

'Yes,' said Melissa with perfect calm, 'It is very different. But in time I am sure I will get used to it. After all, one can get used to anything in time—even some people!'

Very deliberately, she turned away without hurry, to be introduced to someone else. What a nasty, unpleasant woman, she thought to herself, much put out by the encounter. I shall take care not to have anything to do with her in the future. Stephanie pressed her hand in quick approval.

'Maree Chandler deserved that,' she said with satisfaction. 'She is furious because you are so young and pretty. She is frightened of losing her hold over Gareth Caldwell.'

Melissa had no desire to start a conversation about Gareth Caldwell! Quickly, she made her way towards Fred Carstairs.

'You must have been in Altabad for many years to have known my father,' she began cautiously.

'No, my dear. I knew Guy at Fort William in

Calcutta many years ago. I have been in Altabad only three years now.'

'I see,' said Melissa disappointed not to have more information.

'Have you met the old boy yet, the Maharaja?' the Resident asked.

'No,' said Melissa, wondering if this were a tactful change of conversation, 'Not yet. I believe he is unwell. I hope to meet His Highness when he recovers. He has been most generous to me. I am delighted at the prospect of living in my father's house.'

A very wary look came into Fred Carstairs' eyes. 'Er . . . yes,' he said hurriedly. 'You do not find the house too . . . unmanageable for yourself?'

'Not at all,' laughed Melissa, 'It is large, certainly, but I intend to lock up some of the rooms and live only in my father's apartment.'

'I should imagine,' said Fred Carstairs jovially, 'that a pretty young lady such as yourself would prefer the social whirl of London to the solitary pleasures of Koh-i-noor. But then, I presume, curiosity satisfied, you will no doubt return to England shortly?'

Melissa looked him straight in the eye, her head held high. 'No,' she said calmly, 'London's social whirl does not interest me at all. I intend to make Koh-i-noor my permanent home.'

Fred Carstairs looked taken aback and appeared to struggle for words. Then, regaining his composure, he bowed gallantly. 'In that case, London's loss is undoubtedly our gain.'

Melissa observed his impassive face through narrowed eyes. Now, *he* seems not to want me at Koh-i-noor either, she thought in exasperation. Had Gareth

Caldwell started some mysterious conspiracy against her? She was prevented from dwelling on the subject by Dr Herbert who took her arm and drew her aside.

'I must impress upon you, my dear, the necessity for precautions against malaria. The mosquitoes, as you know, proliferate in the east, especially in terrain where there is stagnant water and dense overgrowth. Now the jungle, for instance . . .'

'The jungle,' interrupted Celia suddenly materialising at Melissa's elbow and cutting off her husband mid sentence, 'is beautiful, absolutely beautiful. We must arrange a tiger hunt for your benefit. Would you like that?'

'Oh, I would love it!' exclaimed Melissa, 'My father used to relate to me such thrilling stories about the wild.'

'The man you must meet then,' said Celia, 'is of course Gareth Caldwell. He knows the jungle inside out and he is our champion *shikari*—hunter.'

Melissa was spared the necessity of a reply as Celia Herbert gave an excited shriek.

'Oh, *there* you are, Gareth!' She turned and hurried towards the door, 'Oh, I *am* glad you could come. We were just talking about you.'

Melissa froze for a moment. She dared not turn around to look. Much to her annoyance, her heart began to beat far more rapidly than it had been doing and her throat felt quite dry. She took a long sip of the sherbet and continued to look the other way.

'I promised you I would come,' said Gareth with a languid laugh, in the same mocking tones that seemed to take nothing very seriously. Melissa had no doubt *he* would have no difficulty in pretending they had not met before. But would she?

'Come and meet our lovely young guest of honour, Gareth,' Celia was saying. 'She only arrived from England two days ago.' Melissa closed her eyes and took a deep breath. When she turned to face him, her composure was flawless.

'Melissa, this is Gareth Caldwell, just the man to tell you about the jungle.' He bowed dutifully, his strange, hazel eyes very amused. Dressed in smart, evening dress, he looked very different indeed.

'I am delighted to meet you, Miss Castlewood,' he said without so much as a flicker of an eyelash, 'I hope you will have a pleasant stay in Altabad.' His voice contained just the right mixture of polite interest and—indifference. Melissa could hardly believe that this perfectly groomed, suave playboy, was one and the same as the steely, hard-sinewed man of action she had confronted last night—or, indeed, the immoral villain who pillaged and plundered gentlefolk on the highways. In spite of her earlier resolve, she found herself staring at him wide-eyed with disbelief. Into his golden-coloured eyes leapt a flicker of warning as they hardened momentarily.

But aloud he said, 'I am sure the last thing Miss Castlewood would be interested in, is the jungle. Nasty, damp places quite unsuited to young English girls fresh from home.'

Melissa began to bristle, but retained her poise and smiled sweetly, 'I do not think the jungle is the exclusive preserve of men,' she said, matching his bantering tone.

'No, but it should be. Women generally clutter up

the place with their hairpins and ribbons or get their stockings caught in the bushes just as a man is getting ready to take a shot.'

Melissa was determined not to rise to the bait by showing signs of temper, but had some difficulty in keeping her voice steady. Insufferable man! With an effort, she smiled even more sweetly and said, surprised at her own boldness, 'I see that Mr Caldwell is well acquainted with articles of a lady's apparel! Now, if you will please excuse me . . .' she turned around quickly and walked to the verandah, but not before she had the satisfaction of seeing Gareth Caldwell's face suffuse with colour.

Oh, how she disliked that man! Fanning herself furiously, she strolled into the garden, trying to calm her nerves. Seeing a small, wooden summer house prettily covered with flowering creepers, she went inside and sat down, glad of a few moments' respite. Then, just as she was about to go out again, she heard voices in the garden. The low, throaty laugh she recognised immediately as Maree Chandler's.

'When will we meet again?' she heard Maree ask.

'When I have the time.' Gareth Caldwell! There was no way in which she could leave the summer house without being observed. Ears burning, she sat down again, forced to overhear.

'You are a selfish beast, Gareth,' Maree said petulantly.

'And you, my darling, are a very spoilt woman!'

'You do neglect me dreadfully, Gareth. I have not heard from you for days.'

'I have been busy,' said Gareth shortly.

'Busy! Why, you do nothing except enjoy yourself all day long!' Maree stamped her foot angrily.

'Well,' said Gareth lightly, 'let's just say then I have had a lot of enjoying to do.'

'Not with our new little English-rose heiress, I hope!'

Gareth laughed. 'Oh, come now, Maree! Our little English-rose heiress is hardly my type!'

'Then—shall we meet again next week at the same place?'

Gareth sighed. 'Very well, my dear, spoilt, beautiful Maree, if you insist.'

'Oh, I do, Gareth, I do! Roy is such a dull, uninteresting *bore*. All he can talk about is his wretched diamonds . . .'

'I notice you are not exactly averse to *wearing* them . . .'

The voices moved away into the night. Melissa was appalled at what she had heard. What a despicable cad the man must be! Did he have no morals at all? Making sure that they had gone, seething with indignation, Melissa came out of the summer house and quickly rejoined the other guests. She was greeted by Celia Herbert in a state of high excitement.

'My dear,' she said breathlessly, 'You did not mention that you had been held up by Sher Singh!'

A hush descended upon the drawing room as everyone stopped talking and crowded around Melissa. She bit her lip in a flush of embarrassment and she was aware that her face had turned a bright pink.

'Oh, Melissa,' Stephanie exclaimed, 'How dreadful for you! Did the wretch get away with anything valuable? They say he is such an uncouth villain!'

Melissa was aware of Gareth Caldwell at the far end of the room, leaning indolently on the grand piano next to Maree Chandler, observing her intently, the sardonic half smile never leaving his face.

'Well . . . yes . . .' Melissa found herself stammering, not knowing quite what to say under the hateful gaze. 'That is . . . he . . .' she took a deep breath and pulled herself together. 'He did try to hold up our coach on the way,' she said stiffly, 'but our guards were too quick for him.' The lie did not come easily and she bit her lip again as she heard Gareth laugh lightly. He seemed to be laughing directly at her, almost daring her to reveal his shameful secret!

'But did you *see* him at all, Miss Castlewood?' Milly Patterson asked excitedly. 'He is said to be an evil-looking monster.'

'Oh, indeed he is,' said Melissa, fully recovered, and even daring to cast an impertinent glance in Gareth's direction. 'His face was hooded, of course, but I could tell that he must emanate from the lowest dregs of humanity.'

'The scoundrel needs to be horsewhipped!' declared Tom Patterson heatedly, supported by several of the other men.

'Indeed,' said Gareth blandly, 'when we can catch him, that is!'

The conversation was cut short by the announcement that dinner was served. Melissa went in on the arm of Fred Carstairs who said in a low voice, 'You must let me know if you are ever in need of . . . anything.' He patted her hand kindly. Melissa nodded. More than anything else, she thought to herself,

I am in need of information. But this was neither the time nor the place to ask for it.

Celia Herbert had laid on a lavish buffet table, sparkling with silver cutlery, candles and banks of flowers. White liveried waiters hovered around waiting to be of service as dish upon steaming dish appeared on the table. The conversation became light and general and Melissa found herself the centre of everybody's attention—expect Gareth Caldwell's! His eyes and attention seemed reserved only for Maree Chandler. It appeared strange that Roy Chandler should not take offence at his wife's open interest in another man. But then, women like Maree Chandler were impossible to tame and Roy Chandler, obviously besotted by her, seemed more than content with whatever little she chose to toss in his direction.

Melissa hated to admit it, but Gareth Caldwell's open indifference towards her affected her more than she would have wanted it to. She could not help remembering the feel of his lips on hers and the touch of his hands as they held her face. Even the memory of the incident, trifling and trivial, seemed sufficient to increase the rate of her pulses. She became increasingly angry with herself and retaliated by proceeding to pay Gareth Caldwell back in his own coin. Very studiously, she ignored him for the rest of the evening—but with the sinking suspicion that her indifference meant not a hoot to him!

All the ladies offered their help and advice in the matter of refurbishing Koh-i-noor. Celia and Stephanie offered to collect fabric samples and to arrange for tailors; Milly Patterson said she would send around a house painter whose prices were reasonable; Gordon

Hattersley said a carpenter currently employed at the waterworks would be just the right man to repair the windows and perform other odd works of repair. Someone else knew of a furniture polisher . . .

Melissa was overwhelmed with the kindness and hospitality of everyone present. She would not lack for friends in Altabad—no matter what Mr Gareth Caldwell had to say. She would make a success of her stay in Koh-i-noor, she determined, and make a mockery of all the dreadful lies he had told her . . .

Yet, as she lay on her bed trying to sleep much, much later that night, she could not stop thinking of him. What an amazing double life he led in Altabad— and even more amazing that he should be able to get away with it. Which was the true Gareth Caldwell, the debonair, idle playboy who flirted so outrageously with the lovely Maree Chandler, or the mysterious bandit who thought nothing of flouting Queen and country? It was a dilemma she seemed unable to resolve. But about one fact, she was absolutely clear in her mind. Gareth Caldwell was the most dislikable, insufferable man she had ever met in her life!

CHAPTER
FOUR

DURING the days following the Herberts' party, Melissa found herself completely engrossed in the very satisfying task of putting Koh-i-noor back on its feet. As promised by Milly Patterson, the house painters arrived, as did a host of other workmen. Hafiz's sons, nagged by their father, had set to work in earnest. The entire household began to buzz with activity.

True to their word, Celia and Stephanie proved to be towers of strength, helping Melissa with her shopping, always ready with advice and escorting her endlessly through the quaint but utterly fascinating bazaars of the town. The shops lining the streets on either side, were mostly open in front and raised a little. The goods were displayed on the ground, with the shopkeepers lounging on fluffy white cushions, vociferously extolling the virtues of *their* goods as opposed to their neighbours'. The odd assortment of wares, lying cheek by jowl with each other, took Melissa's breath away with their colourful variety. There were cotton garments, shoes, sandals, edibles, articles of glass, pictures of gods and goddesses, flowers, women's ornaments, earthenware, brass and copper pots, cooking vessels, wooden toys, aromatic *attars*, furniture . . . the array seemed to be unending.

Of particular interest to Melissa was the shop of the *bania*, or the grocer, with its totally unfamiliar collection of foodstuff. Celia, having lived in India for many years, was a fount of information, explaining each item with great patience. Next to the *bania*, was the shop of the sweetmeat -maker with his various confections arranged in large round metal trays, looking like different coloured fudge. Celia explained that most Indian sweets were made of milk, sugar and nuts, with no eggs, as most Indians were vegetarians. Rather daringly, they decided to try one sweet each and Melissa selected a green *barfi* made with pistachio nuts, which she found quite delicious.

In between the exciting shopping expeditions and explorations of the town, Melissa worked from early morning to late at night on her beloved house. Gradually, the atmosphere of Koh-i-noor began to change. It was as if the lonely, loveless house was shaking itself out of its hibernation and coming back to vibrant life. Melissa found herself serenely happy—except for the annoyingly frequent thoughts of Gareth Caldwell!

Since the Herberts' party, she had seen no sign of him. Yet, his nebulous presence was always there. Once or twice she even caught herself wondering idly if he had indeed kept his rendezvous with Maree Chandler and, much to her disgust, she could not suppress the tiny little stabs of jealousy. How absurd! As if she could truly be interested in Mr Insufferable Caldwell—or his lady friends!

She did, however, feel extremely uneasy that she had not reported his evil doings to the authorities but . . . there was some strange force holding her back.

Supposing he *was* telling the truth after all? She lulled herself into believing that it was really best to wait and see what happened next instead of making a hasty decision. Everything at Koh-i-noor seemed so perfect, so tranquil and untroubled.

Until one day, something happened that wrenched her back into a shocked state of reality.

Returning indoors from the garden one afternoon, Melissa paused to speak to Mohan Das near the portico. While he listened to her instructions about the new coach and horses on order, his eyes happened to stray upwards in the direction of the roof. With a sudden oath, he leapt forward, pushed Melissa with all his might and sent her crashing to the ground—at the same instant as two large bricks came hurtling down on to the exact spot where she had been standing. Had she still been there, she would have certainly been gravely injured—even killed!

Without even glancing at her, Mohan Das rushed into the house and up the staircase on his way to the roof. For a moment Melissa lay stunned. Then Zarina rushed at her, sobbing hysterically, and helped her to her feet. Hafiz stood by gaping, his eyes filled with horror. Melissa dusted herself dazedly as Zarina examined her bruised arms, still sobbing loudly.

'I am . . . all right, Zarina,' she reassured her weakly. 'I am not much hurt . . .' Seeing the expression on Hafiz's face, she forced a laugh. 'I must get that . . . that roof wall repaired before there is another . . . accident.'

'No accident, Missy,' Hafiz whispered, 'They try kill you.'

'Nonsense,' said Melissa quickly with far more

confidence than she felt. 'Of course it was an accident. The bricks have been loose since I arrived. It is my fault for not seeing to them earlier.' She turned and hurried into the house, not wishing to encourage any more conversation on the subject.

When she reached her room, she was shaking. For a moment, she sat on the settee, her mind swirling with lightning thoughts. Was it an accident? Or—was someone really trying to kill her? She shook off the thought instantly. But of course, it had to be an accident! For a few moments she paced up and down on the terrace. When she returned to her sitting room, Mohan Das was waiting for her.

'I trust Madam is not hurt?' he asked anxiously. 'I must apologise for my rough behaviour . . .'

Melissa stopped him with a gesture. 'You saved my life, Mohan Das,' she said sombrely, 'I am deeply grateful.'

Mohan Das seemed about to say something but changed his mind. Instead, he managed a wan smile. 'Those bricks need to be repaired. I will see to it immediately.'

'Thank you.' Melissa paused, then asked hesitantly, 'It was . . . an accident, was it not?'

Mohan Das faltered very briefly before replying. 'Of course, Madam. It was an accident.' He bowed, then turned abruptly on his heels and left.

His reassurance left Melissa unsatisfied and the feeling of apprehension remained with her all day. It was as if into the smooth waters of her life, someone had cast a stone . . .

The following day was a Sunday and the Herberts had promised to take Melissa to the neat little whitewashed church where they attended service. An English priest came to Altabad each week from Metapilly to conduct the service. This Sunday, Dr Herbert was to read the lesson.

When they arrived, the church was full and Melissa recognised many people she had met at the Herberts' party. In the front pew, dressed entirely in virginal white, sat Maree Chandler, her jet black hair covered with delicate Brussels lace. She glanced at Melissa only briefly, taking in her simple cotton gown of printed calico, then averted her head rather pointedly. I wonder why she dislikes me so much, Melissa thought to herself—we have nothing in common at all. Which was, of course, quite incorrect. They had Gareth Caldwell in common—although the truth would have probably shocked Melissa had she been aware of it!

Maree Chandler, beautiful as she knew she was, was also only too aware that the full bloom of youth was inexorably passing her by. With every year, more and more effort was needed to maintain those striking looks. Her instinctive dislike of Melissa stemmed from a consuming jealousy. Melissa was not only younger, but also fresh and innocent, her glowing complexion independent of artificial aids. The younger's girl's beauty, her enchanting youth, were too bitter a pill for Maree to swallow. Melissa's sudden arrival on the scene had already proved an imminent threat to her own importance. She was desperately worried in case she lost her own hold over Gareth Caldwell. *She is not my type*, Gareth had said of Melissa, but Maree was far too experienced a woman of the world not to have noticed the look in Gareth's

eyes when he looked at Melissa at the Herberts'
party . . .

Melissa, of course, was completely unaware of the
turmoil she had unknowingly created in the breast of
the older woman. Silently, she kneeled in prayer. She
asked the good Lord to bless her home and reward her
efforts with tranquillity. She felt that, for the first time
in her life, she was in need of a friend whose shoulder
she could lean on and on whom she could place
her burdens of the mind. Inevitably—and annoyingly—into her mind flashed a vision of Gareth's
inscrutable face. Was he the friend she yearned
for?

After the service, as was the custom in Altabad,
everyone gathered at the Club for a game of cricket,
while the ladies sat in the shade of the spreading
banyan trees exchanging domestic chit-chat. There
was a pleasant breeze blowing through the grounds
and luncheon, when it was served on the verandah,
was light and refreshing. There was no sign of Gareth
Caldwell, but over luncheon Melissa found herself
seated next to Roy Chandler. Maree sat at the far end
of the table—possibly in a pointed effort to avoid
her!

'I hope you have not forgotten about my visit to the
mines,' Melissa reminded him, smiling.

'No I have not,' said Roy Chandler genially, 'I had a
word with the Resident about it and he has promised
to issue a permit for you shortly.'

'Are they far from here?' Melissa asked.

'They are about five miles from Altabad town,' he
replied, 'but closer to Koh-i-noor towards the north. I
shall be happy to arrange for your transport and

escort,' he added, 'but do be careful not to wear clothes that are too voluminous or carry any article which may be construed as a receptacle.'

'Oh?' asked Melissa, baffled, 'Why is that?'

'The mines are high security areas,' Roy replied with a twinkle in his eye, 'and we must ensure that no guests ever come under suspicion.'

'But do you mean to say the diamonds can be picked up so casually?' Melissa cried in disbelief.

'Certainly. Workers and officials of the mines have to submit to a thorough search of their clothing before they leave the premises.'

'Oh, how very fascinating!'

'Indeed!' commented Roy Chandler drily, 'Perhaps a shade too fascinating for those blessed with the roving eye!'

'Well,' promised Melissa gaily, 'I shall take good care to stay very clear of your precious diamonds and shall content myself with just looking at them.'

When Melissa returned to Koh-i-noor late in the afternoon, she found a note waiting for her from the Palace. It read: 'Dear Miss Castlewood: I am directed by His Highness to request the pleasure of your company at tea tomorrow afternoon at four p.m. His Highness wishes to inform you that he is now very much better and looks forward to making your acquaintance tomorrow. A carriage has been arranged to fetch you at three p.m.' The letter was signed by an ADC to the Maharaja.

Melissa was immediately excited and very pleased. She had been longing for the opportunity to express her deep gratitude to the man who had opened for her the doors of a new life. Perhaps, there was a great deal to be learned from him as well. He had known her father intimately and would not be averse, maybe, to giving her details about his life—and death.

Much cheered at the prospect of a visit to the Palace, Melissa spent the evening completing her week's accounts. Although she now had sufficient money to cater for her needs at Koh-i-noor, her naturally frugal nature and upbringing made any form of wastage abhorrent and she was determined to spend her money with care.

It was very late at night when Melissa finally closed her ledgers. Getting up from the chair, she stretched luxuriously, yawning and tingling with pleasant tiredness. She dismissed Zarina for the night and went into the bedroom.

Leaning casually against the mantelpiece was Gareth Caldwell.

She felt her heart give a violent leap—a completely unwanted sign of pleasure! But his opening words made her flush with anger.

'Now do you see what a nuisance you are being to everybody?'

She stalked past him rapidly and sat down on the settee, her eyes flaming.

'How, pray, am I being a nuisance to everybody—especially to you?' she asked spiritedly, adding with ice in her tones, 'I had requested you not to make free with my bedroom!'

Gareth shrugged, dismissing her complaint absently. 'There is no other place where I can talk to you in private.'

'Why do you wish to speak to me at all?' she asked

tartly, the sudden memory of his kiss bringing spots of red to her cheeks.

'Because,' he said deliberately, 'somebody tried to . . . harm you today!'

'Rubbish!' Melissa retorted, 'It was an accident.'

'It was not an accident,' said Gareth angrily. 'Can you not get that simple fact into your pretty little head?'

'Mohan Das told me . . .'

'Mohan Das did not wish to alarm you! The fact remains that somebody was sent to Koh-i-noor for the express purpose of disposing of you—and would have done so had it not been for Mohan Das's lightning reflexes. Unfortunately, he got away, whoever he was, before Mohan Das reached the roof.'

All at once, Melissa's shoulders sagged and she buried her face in her hands, all her bravado evaporating like a wisp of smoke in a strong wind. 'Why should anyone wish to harm me,' she said brokenly, her voice muffled and trembling.

'Listen, Melissa,' Gareth came and sat down beside her, unaware that he had addressed her by name, 'Listen to me. I have no desire to frighten you unduly, but your life here is not as it seems. There is a great deal you do not know about Altabad and its intrigues. You must return to England—at least for the time being, or go and stay with friends for a while.'

'*Who* wants to kill me?' Melissa cried in anguish, 'And *why*? Surely, I do have the right to know?'

Gareth observed her silently for a moment through narrowed eyes, as if trying to come to a decision. Then he rose and returned to lean on the mantelpiece.

'Yes,' he said, 'you do have a right to know some of

the answers. It is no longer safe for you to be kept in ignorance.' He paused briefly to take out the pipe tucked in his belt, and lit it. 'Are you aware of your father's work in Altabad?'

Melissa started in surprise. 'I know he was tutor to the young prince.'

'That was not all,' said Gareth quietly. 'His tutoring job was only a cover for his true activities.'

'His true activities?'

'Yes. Colonel Castlewood was on special assignment from the British government to keep an eye on Chand Ram's subversive activities and report them to Headquarters in Calcutta.'

Melissa digested this extraordinary information in bewilderment. 'But . . . but what has all this to do with *me*? I know nothing of these matters!'

'That is not the point! The point is—you are now mistress of Koh-i-noor and in possession of it for life.'

'But why should my house have anything to do with . . . my father's work, or with . . . all this?' She threw her hands up in despair.

This time, Gareth paused significantly before he replied. He seemed uncertain as to how to proceed. He came and sat down again beside her, his face very serious.

'You will probably be surprised to learn exactly what it is that you *have* inherited! Koh-i-noor and the lands attached to it are, perhaps, the most valuable property in all of India today because . . .' he took a deep breath, 'because, they stand on *the richest diamond field yet to be discovered in this state*.'

Melissa stared at Gareth Caldwell, thunderstruck at what he had just said, waiting for him to continue.

'A highly secret survey was carried out on the property when your father was living here. Unfortunately, somebody got wind of the findings.'

'And that was why . . . ?'

'Yes. That was why he had to be removed from the premises. And that is why . . .' Gareth's voice became soft but loaded with menace. 'That is why somebody wants to get rid of you too.'

Melissa sat momentarily stunned, her blood running cold. He spoke with so much earnestness, it was impossible to doubt the truth of his statement.

'Do you know who killed my father?' she asked flatly.

'Yes,' said Gareth, 'I know. The man who administered the poison was not important. He was only a hired assassin. But the brain behind the deed was that of . . . Chand Ram.'

'The Prime Minister?' Melissa had almost known what to expect yet her face was one of shocked surprise.

'Yes,' said Gareth grimly, his face darkening. 'Chand Ram, the sworn enemy of the British. He will do anything to drive the British out of this state. And for this he needs money. The priceless wealth buried under Koh-i-noor is the obvious answer. And you, my little English-rose heiress, are the only obstacle that stands in his way now.'

'But . . . surely he could have seized Koh-i-noor after . . . after my father died?'

Gareth laughed shortly. 'Chand Ram is a wily devil. He dislikes the idea of an open confrontation. Besides, the Maharaja was still powerful and would not have tolerated it. No, Chand Ram's tactics were the old waiting game. The Maharaja is old and ailing and no longer interested in the state since his son died. The legitimate heir is still a very young boy and living very far away. The Maharaja may not have many years left to him. But you . . .' He stopped abruptly.

Something in his voice made Melissa shiver and into her eyes crept a shadow of fear.

'Chand Ram was furious when the Maharaja decided to give you this house. With the Maharaja he is willing to play the waiting game. But with you . . . he will not take any chances.'

Melissa looked at Gareth for a long moment. Then she asked, very softly, '*How do you know all this*?'

This time, he was prepared for the question. His face relaxed into a bland smile. 'I've already told you, my dear girl, that in a profession such as mine, I have to make it my business to know everything. I have my methods.'

'And why,' asked Melissa, her eyes hard, 'should you have any interest in my welfare?'

'Obviously,' said Gareth Caldwell with disarming candour, 'I do not wish my own interests to be affected.'

His own interests! Melissa felt outraged at the cool impudence with which he made the statement.

'In other words, you want me to abandon Koh-i-noor so that you can carry on your criminal activities here undisturbed!'

Gareth pondered the point carefully then replied quietly. 'No. This is *one* of my considerations but not the sole one. I want you to leave Koh-i-noor for your own safety. I would not wish to see you come to harm.'

How coldly impersonal he sounded! Slowly, she sank down on the settee, reeling under the impact of the conversation. Leave Koh-i-noor! Leave her home just when it was beginning to re-awaken out of its long slumber, just when the garden was coming alive with the joys of spring! To return to England, to Cornhill perhaps, to the humiliating life of a companion, or to live alone in London whiling away the days in what Fred Carstairs had called the 'social whirl'! Oh, how pale and insipid it all seemed compared to the living, growing pleasures of Koh-i-noor! Her whole being rebelled at the idea. How dare this . . . this brazen, cold stranger suggest such a thing!

'I will *not* leave Koh-i-noor,' she said, tears of frustration and anger springing to her eyes. 'This is my home, my *only* home! I do not care about diamonds and riches, but I love this house just like my father loved it. I shall *not* be frightened away like a timid mouse scampering back into its hole at the clap of your hands! You, a self confessed *bandit*, a . . . a *traitor* to your country!'

Gareth was totally taken aback by her sudden outburst, then unexpectedly laughed, his voice loaded with mockery. 'Since you know that I am a traitor and a criminal—why have you not reported me to the authorities as you had threatened the other night?' He raised his eyebrows quizzically, his tawny eyes alive with amusement.

Melissa met his gaze only for a brief split second, then lowered her own. 'I don't know,' she whispered miserably, 'I don't know . . .'

'You know of course,' he continued relentlessly, 'that your silence makes you an accessory to whatever crimes I commit?'

'Don't taunt me,' she flared up suddenly, realising full well the truth of what he said, 'or I shall be *driven* to reveal your dreadful secret.'

He considered her with amused mildness, his eyes sure and confident. 'In that case,' he said quite calmly, 'you will find yourself in more trouble than you had bargained for. It is a pity that your intelligence does not match your spirit!'

Melissa pulled herself up to her full height and met his eyes challengingly. 'And it is a pity,' she said bitingly, 'that your manners do not match your prowess at thievery!'

Quite surprisingly, he chuckled with that hateful, sardonic, infuriating chuckle she knew so well by now. 'All right, I apologise for that last statement. I take it back unconditionally. If we are to be on the same side, we shall need to declare at least a truce, if not complete peace.'

Why does he not take anything I say seriously, she fumed inwardly? Aloud she said, 'Tell me—why *did* you hold up my coach when you had no intention of stealing my jewellery?'

Gareth raised an eyebrow at the question. 'Because,' he said coolly, swinging on to the window ledge, 'I wanted to see what you looked like!' Then, with another rapid change of mood, his face became very serious. 'Trust me, Melissa,' he said softly. 'Believe me, I am a friend.'

Melissa's heart stopped beating for a split second at the softness in his voice and the strange, gentle light in his hazel eyes.

'Get Mohan Das to strengthen the latch on this

window,' he said stepping nimbly on to the parapet outside. 'Chand Ram's next attempt may not be as clumsy as his first. That was designed only to frighten you. Next time it may not be so.'

'But then,' she said sweetly, her tone as mocking as his, 'since you consider me to be a partner in crime, I believe that you will be watching over me, will you not?'

She heard him chuckle again softly and then he was gone, slipping into the night like a shadow.

Melissa stared after him for a long while after he had gone. What an enigma Gareth Caldwell was! She could not understand him at all. Could she believe what he had told her? What was his word worth? And yet . . . there was something about his manner that filled her with reassurance. That he was a man of immense cunning she had no doubt. The extraordinary ease with which he appeared to fulfill his double role in Altabad proved him to be a man of unusual daring. Who could believe that the languid, lethargic, pleasure-loving gentleman of leisure and the elusive, ruthless dacoit, Sher Singh, were one and the same?

Not for the first time she wondered—which *was* the real Gareth Caldwell?

CHAPTER
FIVE

BY THE time the Maharaja's coach arrived, promptly
at three in the afternoon, Melissa had had time to mull
over the extraordinary information Gareth had given
her the day before. She couldn't pretend to understand it all yet, but it was certainly disturbing. So
many wheels were now turning at the same time—and
she seemed to be caught in the middle! But Gareth's
presence in the house, in spite of his mysterious
and—at times—arrogant behaviour, filled her with a
strange comfort. *Trust me!* His words kept ringing in
her ears. Dared she trust him? There was so much
about him that was cloaked in mystery. But then, she
really had no choice. He had the edge over her. He
knew everything that she did, but she seemed to know
so little about *his* activities! If she didn't trust him,
who else was there for her in this frightening, alien
and yet so fascinating land?

Zarina's knock on the door, announcing the arrival
of the coach, broke into her reverie sharply. Quickly,
Melissa pulled herself together and looked over herself in the full-length mirror. Long, and full skirted,
the white lace dress with a pale pink bodice did full
justice to her tall, slender figure. With it she wore a
wide-brimmed white bonnet decorated with a small
posy of pink flowers from the garden. She wondered if

she looked all right, her heart fluttering with nervousness. After all, she had never met royalty before! Did one curtsey as in England? Shake hands? Or give the traditional Indian greeting of folded hands? How should she address him? She imagined a long, cold, formal hall lined with stiff courtiers, all resplendent in their blue and gold uniforms and scarlet turban, just like Mohan Das. Oh dear, she thought worriedly, I hope there isn't going to be any fuss and bother. It would be so nice just to be oneself.

She ran down the steps nimbly and climbed into the magnificent carriage. The journey to Altabad town was not very long. The Palace, when it loomed up ahead, took her breath away with its splendid, aristocratic beauty. It was known, she knew, as Lal Mahal—the Red Palace—and now she saw why. The entire building and its sprawling outhouses were of pink sandstone, its turrets and towers caparisoned with flags of the State. It must have hundreds of rooms, she thought to herself wonderingly. How does anyone ever find their way around.

The Palace was surrounded by formal Moghul gardens, landscaped to perfection with beautifully trimmed hedges and banks of carefully cultivated tropical flowers. Here and there, the emerald lawns were dotted with cool flowing fountains, the waters emanating from the open mouths of sylph-like marble figures. The sheer beauty and calm of the vision made Melissa's heart fill with pleasure. Looking at the multicoloured birds flitting through the lush greenery, she could hardly believe that this placid, pastoral facade of sylvan beauty concealed behind it so many horrible evils . . .

A dozen uniformed guards sprang to attention as the shining black carriage came to a halt in the elaborate porch overhung with clusters of magenta bougainvillaea. Through the wide open, stately doors of carved wood, she could see the entrance hall, resplendent with sparkling chandeliers of the purest Belgian glass crystal. She might have been an important State delegation being received with so much pomp and ceremony! Melissa felt her nervousness return as the butterflies started up again in the region of her stomach.

She was now escorted through what appeared to be miles of corridors, all encased within shining black and white marble, thickly carpeted and with chandeliers every few yards. On and on they seemed to go, up staircases, wide and sweeping, down others, turning this way and that until she felt she would never be able to find her way back if she needed to do so alone. Just as she was beginning to wonder if they would ever arrive at their destination, the guards escorting her stopped. One stepped forward to part the heavy scarlet drapes that covered a massive door, which now opened at once.

Melissa stepped forward and found herself confronted with a tall, stiff gentleman with a thick black moustache and beard. He bowed.

'I am the aide-de-camp to His Highness, who awaits you in his private sitting room. Please follow me.'

Melissa smiled in response, then looked round. They were in a room so large that she was not sure where it ended! It was exquisitely furnished with soft, muted colours and priceless carved wooden and brass furniture. On display were enormous oil paintings,

marble statuary and obviously very valuable antiques.
On the floor lay thick pile Persian carpets of intricate
designs. This was evidently the formal drawing room
attached to the Maharaja's suite, where he enter-
tained official visitors. She felt privileged to be received by him in his private sitting room.

At the far end of the drawing room, the aide-de-
camp opened a door. 'Miss Melissa Castlewood, Your
Highness,' he announced, then stood aside to allow
her to enter.

The room was much smaller than the one they had
just passed through and it was furnished for comfort
rather than formal display. The windows were curtained with gay, chintz drapes. In a corner stood a
carved desk littered with papers, books and writing
materials. In another corner was a large, comfortable
sofa set upholstered in leather with a low table in front
of it.

On the sofa, almost submerged by the enormous
cushions, sat a small, frail looking man with a heavily
lined face. Melissa stared at him, wide-eyed and
nervous, then slowly folded her hands in the traditional Indian greeting. For a brief moment the old man
said nothing. Then he smiled and his face lit up with
pleasure.

'Melissa Castlewood! My dear, how many years
you take me back!' He patted the sofa and said,
'Come. Come and sit next to me and let me feast my
tired, old eyes on your lovely face, my child.'

Melissa did as he asked, lowering her eyes demurely. She felt his eyes search her face as if looking for
something. 'You must forgive me for staring, my
child,' he said softly, 'but I feel I must gaze my fill

upon the face of the daughter of my dearest friend, Guy Castlewood.' His voice shook with emotion and, as Melissa looked up at him, she was astonished and very moved to see tears in his eyes.

He stretched his thin, bony hand and took hers in it. 'I have been waiting for this moment for many years, my dear. How I wish your dear father could have been with us! What would I not give to have my precious friend with me again, especially now when I need him so badly.'

Suddenly, Melissa felt her nervousness vanish as a lump rose to her throat, deeply touched by the longing and loneliness in the old man's voice.

'So have I been waiting for this moment, Your Highness,' she said gently. 'I do not have the words to thank you for everything that you have been doing for me. You have changed the entire course of my life and given me so much that I could never have dreamed of possessing.'

'My dear Missy,' he began, then, seeing her expression of surprise at his use of the name, he smiled. 'That is what Guy always called you when he talked about you and about all the things he was going to give you when you grew up and joined him in India.' He paused and sighed deeply. 'But things were not to be as we had planned.' He brushed a silent tear from his eye with a frail, shaking hand. Melissa felt the tears well up in her own eyes and coughed hastily to clear her throat. It would not do to depress this dear old man further with her own tears.

'What has happened, has happened,' she said with forced briskness. 'We must not think of the past.'

The Maharaja smiled sadly. 'For old people like

me,' he said quietly, 'There is only the past. But for you . . . for you, my dearest Missy, I want to see that there is only the future.' Then, changing the mood of sadness, he asked suddenly, 'And tell me, how do you like your new home? Are you as happy in Koh-i-noor as Guy always was?'

'Oh yes, Your Highness,' Melissa cried, 'I am *very* happy in Koh-i-noor! It is a beautiful house, full of charm and comfort such as I have never known. I am beginning to love it dearly. Thank you for giving it to me. I shall cherish it always.'

A sudden cloud passed over the Maharaja's face. He seemed to be at a loss for words. Then, very hesitantly, he asked, 'And . . . all is . . . well at the house? You are not . . . troubled in any way?'

Melissa hesitated fractionally before answering with bright cheerfulness, 'No, I am not troubled in any way at all.' Determined not to say too much to worry the old man, she looked him straight in the eye. He smiled and patted her hand. 'Good. And how are you spending your days at Koh-i-noor?'

'My days seem to be fully occupied, Your Highness, for there is a great deal to do in the house.' She related to him all the improvements she was planning, describing the garden in detail, asking his advice here and there. She felt astonishingly relaxed with the gentle old man with the sad, brown eyes. It was as if she had known him all her life, so easily did the conversation flow.

But it was about her father that she yearned to know and at the first opportunity that presented itself, she said, 'I have known so little about my father's life in Altabad, but I seem to have always had the impression that he was happy here.'

She noticed immediately that a wary look came into
the gentle, brown eyes. The Maharaja nodded. 'Yes,
Guy was always happy in Altabad. He loved Koh-i-
noor, you know.'

'I know,' she said, 'his eyes used to shine when he
spoke of it to me.'

'Just as,' said the old man softly, 'yours are doing
now!'

Melissa lowered her head shyly. 'It is the only home
I have ever known. Perhaps my father felt the same
way for that very reason.'

A sudden sadness came over the deeply-lined face
and into his eyes flashed a shadow of fear. He frowned
and shook his head. 'I hope I have not made a
mistake,' he whispered. 'Guy will never forgive me if I
have!'

'A mistake, Your Highness?' Melissa was puzzled
by the phrase.

But the Maharaja shook his head quickly, then
forced a smile. 'It is time for tea, I think. I have
ordered for you some fresh scones with jam and some
cakes and sandwiches. I am sure you must be missing
your English delicacies.'

'Thank you,' said Melissa, very touched, 'I must
confess I am very partial to scones.'

The Maharaja leaned forward and pressed a bell on
the table. Immediately, the door opened and a footman appeared. He gave an order then turned again to
Melissa.

'And now, my dear Missy, you must tell me about
your life in England and your impressions of my
country.'

'I would be pleased to, Your Highness.' While they waited for tea to be served, she described to him the people in Cornhill, her duties in the house, the happy schooldays at Miss Fenton's, the loneliness that engulfed her every time she received a letter from her father. He listened very intently, making occasional comments in order to clarify some detail.

Finally, she stopped with a laugh. 'I have been doing all the talking Your Highness. What *I* would really like to do is to learn more about my father's life in Altabad.'

Again, the same wariness crept into the old man's eyes. He patted her hand affectionately. 'We will have plenty of occasions to talk, my dear. In time, you shall know all there is to know. But for the moment it is best to remember that at the Palace, even the walls have ears.' He had lowered his voice to a whisper and again, his eyes were clouded. 'Do not let anything frighten you, Missy. You are well . . . protected.'

Protected! Then Gareth Caldwell had been telling the truth—her life *was* in danger! But then . . . did the Maharaja know about Gareth Caldwell and his mysterious doings as Sher Singh? A thousand questions made ready to tumble from Melissa's lips, but before she could voice them, the door opened and tea was announced, making further questions inadvisable.

Over the delightful English tea the Maharaja had so thoughtfully ordered for her, the conversation veered to general topics. With two footmen in constant attendance, there was no opportunity for anything else. She asked after his grandson and immediately his face lit up.

'I am told he is growing up to be a fine young man,' he said with obvious pride. He chuckled. 'The rascal wants an Arab stallion for his birthday next month.'

'And are you going to send him one?' she asked.

'It is already on its way to . . . where he is.' For a moment Melissa thought he was going to say more but instead he sighed and muttered almost under his breath, 'I would give anything to have him with me here.'

'Maybe you will one day,' said Melissa quickly, also in a low voice which could not be heard by the footmen.

The Maharaja nodded and sighed again. 'Perhaps. But in the meantime, I also have a gift for you. Your father once mentioned that you were beginning riding lessons at your school in England.'

'Yes,' said Melissa. 'I love horses. I won the school prize in show jumping on a horse called Hyperion,' she added shyly.

'In that case, I have made the right choice of a gift. It is my favourite mare, a dapple grey called Roshni— light.'

'Oh, Your Highness, you have already given me so much! I cannot impose on your generosity any more!'

'My dear Missy,' the old man said gently, 'there are few pleasures left to me now in life. Giving you what Guy would have wanted to, is one of them. You must not deprive me of it.'

Melissa was very moved. 'You will spoil me with your kindness,' she said, 'but if it gives you pleasure, I accept with gratitude.'

They sat in silence while the footmen cleared the

tea dishes. It was only after they had withdrawn that the Maharaja spoke again.

'There was a time, my child, when there was much laughter in these rooms. Now there is only . . . evil. You must bring the laughter back again. Your father is no longer with us, cut down by the hand of a villain. But his spirit lingers, waiting to be avenged . . . I feel it . . . *I feel it* . . .' His voice trembled with emotion as he clasped Melissa's hand with his bony fingers. She stared at him, disturbed at the intensity of his emotion, but before she could reply, the door opened and the ADC appeared. He bowed and announced. 'His Excellency, the Prime Minister.' He stood aside as Chand Ram stepped into the room.

Beside her, she felt the Maharaja tense and into his face came an expression of deep distaste. His manner became coldly formal. As Chand Ram stood before him and bowed, he waved him into a chair.

'Miss Castlewood,' the Maharaja said, his voice low but steady, 'May I present to you His Excellency the Prime Minister of Altabad?'

Chand Ram bowed again, then leaned forward and took Melissa's hand in his own. His grip was firm. He lowered his head and brushed the top of her hand with his lips. It was all Melissa could do to suppress the wave of repulsion that swept through her.

'I am honoured,' said Chand Ram in a voice that was very deep and very smooth, 'to be meeting the daughter of the late Colonel Castlewood. He was, indeed, a true friend to us.' Slowly, with an expression of sorrow, he sank down into the chair. Momentarily, Melissa felt sickened by the man's duplicity, so decided to say nothing. The Maharaja had withdrawn into his shell like a frightened snail and sat examining his nails in frigid silence.

Unperturbed by the tension he had created around him, Chand Ram said easily, 'Altabad has a great deal to thank Colonel Castlewood for. His tragic illness, cutting him off in the prime of his life, left his friends in Altabad shattered. You have my very deep sympathies, Miss Castlewood.'

With some difficulty, Melissa quelled the nausea in her throat and smiled forcedly. 'Thank you, Your Excellency,' she said coolly, 'I am touched by your sentiments.' I must not show him that I am in any way disturbed by him, she told herself sternly. I must retain all my poise. There was, therefore, no way in which Chand Ram could have guessed the turbulence in her heart as she faced him with supreme serenity.

'And you, Miss Castlewood,' he asked, 'are you enjoying your stay at Koh-i-noor?'

'Indeed, I am,' she replied with a bright smile. 'It is a beautiful house but much needs to be done.'

'I am told you have already wrought many miracles in its appearance,' Chand Ram said, rubbing his chin thoughtfully. He turned to the Maharaja as the old man asked a question about a matter of administration and, while they conversed, Melissa found the opportunity to study the man who was so implacably her enemy.

Chand Ram was a big man by every standard, built like an ox with broad shoulders and a ramrod straight figure. His face was adorned by a well-trimmed moustache and he wore his hair combed back and well oiled with pomade. There were streaks of grey here and there but, from his face, it was impossible to tell his age. He could have been anywhere between fifty and seventy! His small black eyes, set closely on either side of a hook nose, were piercing. On one cheek was a black mole. He wore a white uniform, immaculate and stiffly starched and around his ample waist was a scarlet cummerbund. He was obviously a man of some refinement, suave and extremely well groomed. The impression he gave was one of confident power and, involuntarily, Melissa felt a slight shudder pass through her.

Having completed his talk with the Maharaja, Chand Ram rose and bowed again. 'I shall leave you to continue your chat with His Highness. I am sure there are many matters you wish to discuss. But I do look forward to the opportunity of meeting you again. I wish you a happy stay in Altabad—and in Koh-i-noor.' His look was enigmatic. Half way to the door he paused and looked back.

'I trust that you will stay for some time amidst us, Miss Castlewood?'

Melissa smiled with all the sweetness she could muster. 'Indeed, I hope to, Your Excellency. Altabad—and Koh-i-noor—have so many pleasures to offer.'

'Good,' he exclaimed, 'Good. In that case, we shall certainly meet again.' With another imperceptible bow, he opened the door and went out.

For a moment after his departure, there was silence. The Maharaja's face was drawn and extremely tense. He fidgeted restlessly, then rose to his feet with the help of a walking stick.

'Come, my dear,' he said abruptly, 'let me show you the pride of my life—my books. Alas, my eyes are

not what they used to be. I have great difficulty in
reading.'

'Perhaps,' said Melissa with sincerity, 'you will
allow me to read to you sometimes?'

His face showed signs of genuine pleasure. 'I would
be delighted but . . . would not the company of a tired
old man bore you, my dear?'

'Not at all, Your Highness,' Melissa protested
quickly. 'It would give me great pleasure indeed. We
have both suffered tragic personal losses,' she ventured, 'perhaps that will be a good basis for
friendship.'

He looked visibly moved and his eyes became
misty. 'Yes,' he nodded, 'perhaps it will. You will
take the place of the son I had and lost.'

The next hour was spent pleasantly in the Maharaja's enormous library filled with books and documents of every description. There were rare manu-
scripts in Sanskrit that he showed her, explaining each
one in detail, his face alive and animated. His collection of English books was vast, ranging in subject
matter from history and biography, to science and
literature. It was decided that one day the following
week Melissa would come and read to him in the
afternoon and again stay for tea.

The discussion about the books had chased away
much of the earlier tension in both and by the time
Melissa made to leave, she felt pleasantly relaxed.
The Maharaja was a fount of information on many
subjects and she discovered that he was extremely
well-informed about all parts of the world. Leaning
heavily on his walking stick, he escorted her to the
door of his sitting room. Very impulsively and sur-

prised at her own boldness, Melissa bent forward and kissed him lightly on the cheek. His face lit up with startled pleasure. He stroked her hand affectionately.

'We will be friends,' he said quietly, 'we both need someone to love and be loved by.' Then, putting his face close to hers he whispered with unexpected suddenness, 'Do not trust Chand Ram, my dear. And . . . take care.'

He had moved his face away before Melissa realised what he had said. Through the open door she saw the ADC waiting to escort her out. Confused for a moment by the Maharaja's words, she looked startled, but, at a warning sign from him, refrained from further comment.

On the long way back down the corridors and staircases, Melissa was lost in thought. It had been painful to see the Maharaja, once a powerful ruler, reduced to such loneliness. It was almost as if he no longer had the desire to carry on with life. He had mentioned her father frequently in their conversation, but briefly and only in passing. It was as if the subject caused him too much pain to be brought into the open. But, thought Melissa, there will be other opportunities. We both need a friend; we shall fulfill the need in each other.

They were walking down a paved path on the way to the waiting carriage when Melissa, immersed in her own thoughts, missed a step and stumbled badly. She did not fall, but a quick pain shot through her ankle as she tried to put it on the ground. She winced and bit her lip. Oh dear, she thought irritably, what a nuisance!

Almost immediately, two liveried servants came running up behind her, carrying between them a chair with sturdy arms. One of the servants bowed and said, 'His Excellency is most distressed to have witnessed Madam's mishap. I am commanded to carry Madam to His Excellency's apartments so that the Palace physician may be summoned.'

Melissa was about to refuse politely when, raising her head, she observed Chand Ram himself standing in a balcony overlooking the gardens. Catching her eye, he bowed. Even at that distance, Melissa could feel the magnetic power of his gaze. Her willpower wavered. Meekly, without a word, she climbed into the chair.

The Prime Minister was waiting for her at the entrance of his first floor apartment. On hand were two maidservants to assist her dismount from the chair and settle comfortably in a green brocaded sofa, while Chand Ram fussed around barking instructions. The presence of the maidservants reassured Melissa. Certainly he would not try to harm her in any way on his own premises.

Half reclining on the sofa, she watched him in silence, once again very aware of the force of authority the man radiated. She was almost afraid to look into his eyes. But, look into them she must. Outwardly, Chand Ram was the picture of anxious concern for her as he bustled around offering suggestions. For a moment he left the room to fetch her a special liniment to apply on the ankle while waiting for the physician to arrive. Melissa looked around her curiously.

The vast salon was overwhelming in its opulence.

There were exquisite antique treasures everywhere interspersed with sparkling crystal glass ornaments and Chinese porcelain *objets d'art*. There were rich, embroidered silks and satins shot with gold thread with chairs upholstered in heavy purple damask.

By the time Chand Ram returned with the medication, Melissa was more at ease, having had time to regain her composure. It was a curious situation and one that, she realised, she must handle with tact. If she were to get the better of this man, she must not show the slightest sign of fear. Chand Ram was not aware of everything she knew. That was her protection for the moment. She wondered what Gareth Caldwell would have to say if he could see her now, so cosily ensconced in the den of the man who was out to kill her!

Under the circumstances, there was only one thing left to do. Very deliberately, Melissa set about the task of disarming her enemy . . .

'How very kind of you, sir,' she said smiling brightly as she took the bottle of liniment Chand Ram handed her. 'I fear I am being a nuisance to you by keeping you from important matters of State.'

He smiled benignly with an attempt at modesty. 'Alas, Miss Castlewood, I am burdened with many problems but I deem it an honour to be of service to the daughter of a man for whom I felt nothing but unbounded admiration.'

Not by the flicker of an eyelash did Melissa reveal her feeling of revulsion for the man. He is vain, she thought cannily, and what every vain man likes is flattery!

'What exquisite taste you have, Your Excellency,'

she exclaimed, her eyes roving round the room in admiration. 'Every object pleases the senses.'

'I am an inveterate traveller,' said Chand Ram, expanding visibly, 'I enjoy collecting objects of beauty. I am pleased that my modest efforts meet with your approval.'

A knock on the door announced the arrival of the physician who proceeded to examine her foot immediately with great competence.

'Fortunately, Madam,' he said, 'it is only a minor sprain. I shall prescribe a poultice which will bring you relief by tomorrow.'

Melissa was relieved to hear the diagnosis. There was so much to be done at Koh-i-noor that the last thing she wanted was to be laid up in bed with a silly ankle complaint. The physician prepared the poultice and applied it, bandaging the ankle with firmness. As he left and Melissa made a move to rise, Chand Ram stopped her with a gesture.

'Perhaps,' he said cordially, 'you would care to share a glass of sherry with me before you leave?'

Melissa hesitated but only briefly. However unpleasant the prospect of spending time with him was, she must not forget that, in order to defeat him, she had to get to know him better. Fluttering her eyelashes demurely, she agreed, murmuring, 'I should love to, Your Excellency. I *adore* sherry.' Which was not, of course, strictly true, but then in love and war everything was considered fair. And this, she determined grimly, was going to be war!

As she sipped delicately, she chattered on mindlessly, making small talk, playing on his vanity and setting the seal on her own wide-eyed innocence.

Gradually, Chand Ram's tone of oily courtesy changed to one of overt self-appreciation. It was with difficulty that Melissa retained the expression of awe and admiration. She listened attentively, her eyes nevertheless taking in all the little details of the chamber and the rooms beyond. Why she was taking a secret inventory of his apartment, she did not know; but, perhaps, one day the information would come in useful. In any case, she had learned two important traits of her adversary—he drank heavily and he was excessively vain.

The ankle was by now well enough to support her weight if she were careful, but Chand Ram insisted she should not try to walk to the coach. The chair was summoned again and she quickly said her goodbyes.

'You are a gentleman of rare qualities, Your Excellency,' she purred. 'I cannot express the pleasure I have felt in listening to your illuminating conversation. Thank you for your help in my stupid accident.'

Chand Ram bowed. 'The pleasure has been mine, my dear, dear Miss Castlewood. Perhaps one day next week you will do me the great honour of dining with me?'

'We shall see,' said Melissa cheerfully, privately shuddering at the thought. 'Goodbye and thank you again.'

It was not until she was comfortably seated in the carriage and speeding away towards home, that Melissa heaved a profound sigh of relief and sank back into the cushions, exhausted at the effort of the past two hours. Nevertheless, she could not help feeling a stab of triumph. Not only was she beginning to know the man behind her father's murder, but she realised the great advantage she had over him. She knew that he was her enemy—but he had no idea that she was his!

It was an unpleasant, dangerous escapade she was undertaking, but she refused to let herself waver from her determination to encourage Chand Ram's attentions if this was the only way to bring him down. I am playing with fire, she thought to herself grimly. I know nothing of politics and intrigue! But she had no other weapon with which she could fight this man who had snuffed out the life of her darling Papa. He had to be conquered—and Papa's murder had to be avenged!

CHAPTER
SIX

IT WAS already dark by the time Melissa got back to Koh-i-noor. Slowly, with the help of Zarina, much distressed at the accident, Melissa climbed up the stairs into her apartment.

'I am not very hungry, Zarina,' she said, opening the door to her bedroom, 'but I do feel a little tired. I shall nap for an hour after which perhaps you would be kind enough to fetch me a bowl of vegetable broth.'

She hobbled into her room and turned up the lamp burning on the desk. As the room flooded with light and she turned towards the bed, she gasped. Reclining on her settee, munching an apple, was Gareth Caldwell!

She stared at him in astonishment as her heart gave an irritating little leap. 'I see,' she said frostily, sitting down in a chair and facing him, 'that these visitations are becoming quite a habit!' She hoped she had succeeded in keeping the pleasure out of her voice.

He continued eating the apple, paying scant attention either to her or to what she had just said. Then, he aimed the core of the eaten apple out of the window, wiped his hands on his handkerchief and stood up. He looked at her sternly.

'What do you mean by consorting with Chand Ram in his private apartments?' he asked sharply.

Melissa was stung by the insolence of his tone, surprised in spite of herself, at how he had managed to hear about her little adventure in so short a period of time. 'I was not aware,' she replied, bristling, 'that my doings are subject to your approval! In any case, I was not "consorting", as you so delicately put it, with Chand Ram. I hurt my foot in the Palace compound and went up to the apartments to await the physician. Or did your spies forget to tell you that?'

'You didn't have to linger over a glass of sherry, did you?' he persisted churlishly. 'Don't you have any common sense at all?'

Furious, Melissa staggered painfully to her feet, trying to draw herself up to her full height. 'I have far more common sense than you have courtesy, obviously,' she said icily. 'My father used to say, before attacking your enemies, you must get to know them. How can I fight Chand Ram and bring him to book unless I know something about the man and his tactics?'

Gareth stared at her for a brief moment in utter astonishment, then, much to her disgust, threw back his head and shook with muted laughter. 'You plan to fight Chand Ram on your own, do you?' he spluttered, his face contorted with sardonic amusement. 'And, pray, how precisely do you intend setting about that?'

Suddenly, the anger went out of Melissa and she sat down again weakly. 'I don't know,' she said helplessly, shaking her head, 'I don't know. But I know I have to try everything that I can think of.'

For a moment, he said nothing. Then he began to pace up and down. 'Chand Ram is a devil, Melissa,' he said in a gentler tone of voice. 'There is more to him than you can ever learn. You will not be able to even make a dent in his thick hide, no matter what you try. You will only end up making a fool of yourself—and making more trouble for me than it is worth. Can't you see that?'

'Then what am I supposed to do?' she cried in protest, 'Sit back and wait for him to kill me?'

'No,' said Gareth thoughtfully, 'But I have asked you to trust me. Can't you leave it at that? In any case,' he said shortly, 'I don't want you to meet him again. I don't like the idea of you even in the same room as Chand Ram.'

Something in his voice made Melissa look up at him in astonishment. Her heart gave a quick flutter at the thought that crossed her mind. Gareth Caldwell was jealous! Unaccountably, her heart soared with a sudden, perverse pleasure. She looked at him, wide-eyed, and smiled sweetly, enjoying the situation.

'The Prime Minister has invited me to dine with him next week. Should I not go, then?'

Gareth's lips set tight. 'You would be a fool to go,' he said tersely, 'I absolutely forbid it!'

Melissa raised her eyebrows in mock surprise. '*Forbid* it?' her voice was incredulous. 'And pray who are you to enforce your will on me?'

Gareth's face suddenly became very serious. 'Don't play games with Chand Ram,' he said very quietly. 'You will not be able to accept the rules according to which Chand Ram plays. However,' he walked across to the window and slung one leg across the sill, 'if you insist on cutting your own throat, do go ahead. I don't really give a damn.' He leapt lightly on to the parapet outside and was gone.

For a long moment, Melissa stared after him. Had she gone too far with Gareth, she wondered in dismay. Perhaps she had been wrong to goad him into a temper. He was right, after all. There was no way in which she could fight Chand Ram on her own. But then, couldn't he see that she could be of help to him as well? Why was the man so arrogant? If *only* he weren't such an *attractive* devil!

Annoyed, depressed and confused, Melissa changed quickly into her night gown and lay down in bed, exhausted. She could no longer deny that she was beginning to fall in love with Gareth Caldwell and the realisation infuriated her. It was obvious he felt nothing towards her except a sense of protection because of his own selfish interests. He treated her like a child! And yet . . . she could not but help remember the unexpectedly soft look in his eyes as he had bid her goodnight yesterday. What an impossible bundle of contradictions the man was, she thought crossly. Would she ever be able to understand him?

After a day's rest, Melissa's ankle felt so much better, she ventured round the garden for a slow walk. Hafiz and his sons were hard at work, hoeing, digging, weeding and watering. After the rains, she knew, the garden would be in full bloom again. The blue jacaranda trees were covered with blossoms as were the bright yellow laburnums and the pink acacia. The grass had been cut and the red brick paths stood out in bold relief. It was indeed a pleasing sight and Melissa felt a surge of contentment replace the confused depression of the previous night.

To revive her spirits completely, the following day brought her precious gift from the Maharaja—Roshni, the beautiful dapple grey mare. Melissa was utterly enchanted with her. Her coat shone with careful grooming as she held her head high in the air and neighed softly. As Melissa touched her nose, she nuzzled her head against her shoulder, her large, liquid eyes very gentle. The mare was already saddled and scratched the ground with a hoof as if impatient to be on her way. Melissa could hardly wait to get into the saddle. She went to her room and quickly wrote back a warm letter of thanks to the Maharaja, promising to visit him again as soon as he sent word. She handed the letter to the groom who had accompanied Roshni and prepared to mount.

'Madam wishes to go riding?' asked Mohan Das, observing the scene silently so far.

'Why, yes,' said Melissa. 'My ankle is so much better and I cannot think of a greater pleasure than exploring the countryside on my beautiful Roshni.'

'If Madam would kindly wait a few minutes, I shall fetch my horse and accompany Madam,' he said making a move to go.

'No,' said Melissa firmly, 'That will not be necessary, Mohan Das. I am sure I will not . . . get lost. I am beginning to know the area well by now.'

Mohan Das hesitated and frowned. 'Nevertheless,' he said calmly, 'I will follow at a discreet distance. Madam will not be troubled by my presence.' He turned resolutely and strode towards the stables where his own horse was tethered.

Melissa made a grimace but did not argue. Gareth Caldwell again! Obviously, Mohan Das had instructions not to let her out of his sight, especially in the open. As she expertly swung into the saddle, she looked down on the wonderfully green and placid countryside that surrounded Koh-i-noor, basking now in the spring sun. As if Chand Ram would dare attack her in broad daylight! Surely Gareth Caldwell was carrying matters too far! With a toss of her hair she dug her stirrups gently into the mare's sides. Immediately, Roshni took off in a determined trot, soon breaking into a gallop as they reached the open road. She heard the sound of Mohan Das's horse behind her but decided to ignore it. After about a mile she knew there was a path through the forest which led out into the open fields. Determined not to allow Mohan Das's proximity to trouble her, she turned off the main road and threaded her way carefully through the trees until she again came out into the open.

It was a memorable ride. The saddle felt as if it had been designed for her and Roshni responded not only to her touch but also to her every mood. As she galloped through forests and fields and alongside the river, Melissa's heart soared with pure joy. She felt as if her spirits had been let loose to fly as they wished in the vast expanse of sky above and an immense sense of freedom engulfed her. As she flew by, the creatures of the wild scampered into the undergrowth, watching her with wide, surprised eyes. Wild deer, peacocks, groups of gibbering monkeys and birds of vibrant plumage were all around in profusion as she sped past.

Eventually, tired but tingling with happiness, her

face flushed and glowing, she arrived back at Koh-i-
noor to be followed a few moments later by a flustered
Mohan Das,

'Madam rides very fast,' he gasped breathlessly,
dismounting and wiping his face drenched with perspiration, 'It is not advisable.'

'Nonsense!' retorted Melissa but not unkindly, 'As
you can see, Mohan Das. I did not get lost and am
perfectly at home in a saddle.'

Mohan Das bowed with a faint smile, 'Indeed,
Madam is proficient as a horsewoman but,' he paused
fractionally, 'it is not Madam's prowess in the saddle
that is in question.' Dutifully, he led the horses away
towards the stables.

From that day on, Melissa began to rise at dawn
every morning, determined not to miss her daily ride
on Roshni. Reluctantly, Mohan Das continued to
follow her, always maintaining a careful distance but
strongly disapproving of her habit.

Early in the following week, Melissa received
another note from the Maharaja's aide-de-camp, inviting her to spend the afternoon with His Highness,
to read to him and to stay to tea. The old man again
received her with much pleasure. They sat in the
comfortable library and she read to him for an hour
from *The Pickwick Papers*, chuckling over the amusing passages. Later, over tea, he asked, 'And how is it
that a pretty young lady like you has escaped the
attentions of an ardent suitor?'

Melissa blushed and shook her head. 'There were
hardly any ardent suitors in Cornhill,' she said wryly.

'And what about Altabad? Is there no one here that
has caught your fancy?' he persisted.

Melissa hastily averted her head to hide the growing warmth in her cheeks. 'I am far too occupied with setting my house in order to be much concerned with gentlemen at the moment.'

'You have, I take it, had the occasion to meet young Gareth Caldwell?' the Maharaja asked unexpectedly, 'I understand the gentleman is not only very presentable, but also a good sportsman and a man of private means?' Was there a twinkle somewhere in those regal eyes?

'Yes . . . I believe I have . . .' Melissa replied, much flustered. She quickly poured herself and the Maharaja a second cup of tea, wondering whether the question had any more significance than appeared on the surface. Did the Maharaja know of Gareth's amazing double life? His hideout at Koh-i-noor? She longed to ask, but dared not. There were moments when the old man's eyes were surprisingly canny and she had the feeling he knew much more than he was prepared to admit.

'Do tell me about the old days in Altabad, Your Highness,' she said in an effort to divert the trend of conversation and knowing how nostalgic he was about the past. 'I am told there is to be a tiger hunt shortly, for a man-eater that has been ravaging some outlying villages. I know so little about *shikar* and would be grateful for some instruction.'

The remainder of the afternoon was spent in pleasant reminiscing and by the time Melissa left, her charming host was once again in high spirits, much cheered by her lively, inquisitive company.

For the past few days, Melissa had seen nothing of

Gareth Caldwell. But, in the meantime, there had been much excitement because the carriage of no less a person than Fred Carstairs had been held up late one night and the British Resident had been deprived of his gold watch and chain and a signet ring of great value. There was great indignation among the British community, it was said, and Carstairs himself was hopping mad. It was rumoured that he had already requested a posse of superior British troops from Fort St George in Madras for a fresh offensive against Sher Singh's gang.

Melissa was greatly apprehensive at the news and at the prospect of the hideout at Koh-i-noor being discovered, and, she had to admit, especially at the prospect of Gareth himself being caught. Side by side, was a feeling of intense irritation. Surely Gareth had better sense than to humiliate the British Resident himself? Was it necessary to *ask* for more trouble than he already had—and place *her* in a position of such vulnerability? But she had no idea where to locate him at the moment. However, her heart leapt when Tom Patterson sent her a message asking if she would like to participate in the tiger hunt scheduled for the coming weekend. Gareth Caldwell, he mentioned in his note, was to be one of the guns.

The hunting party was not very large, consisting of only two other guns, those of Tom Patterson and young Nigel Bannister. Celia Herbert disliked the jungle and so had opted out, Milly Patterson was away in the hills of the Nilgiris, and so Melissa had only Stephanie Herbert for female company.

The men had already left on horseback the night before and had spent the night at the hunting lodge which was to be their base, organising the beaters for the early morning. So as not to miss the first light, Melissa and Stephanie started out to join them while it was still dark, travelling by coach since there was a reasonably good road going all the way to the lodge. Melissa's heart bounded with excitement as, on arrival in the pale gloom of dawn, she saw the line of elephants waiting and ready to carry them into the depth of the jungle in search of the deadly man-eater. The elephants were beautifully caparisoned, each with a sitting platform laced to its back and a *mahout* perched precariously on the swaying head. Melissa was enchanted at the sight and not at all nervous since she knew that a jungle ride on elephant back was completely safe. The denizens of the wild accepted the elephant as a fellow inhabitant and the fact that the pachyderm carried passengers on its back very often missed their notice.

The lodge, on stilts and made entirely of heavy logs of teak wood, was utterly delightful, set in a clearing surrounded by lush greenery. In the early morning light, it looked like a haven of tranquillity, even with the hustle and bustle going on in preparation for the shoot.

As Melissa looked around anxiously for Gareth Caldwell—who was nowhere to be seen!—Stephanie clutched her arm. 'Look who is here,' she whispered, pointing towards the wooden verandah that ran round the lodge. Melissa raised her head and gave a gasp of dismay. Draped very gracefully over the verandah rails, looking absolutely stunning in a dress of crisp white organdie with an elaborately embroidered bodice and a sash of blue satin, was Maree Chandler!

Momentarily dismayed, Melissa's eyes stole down to her own rather simple choice of an undistinguished green printed cotton with neither frill nor flounce, selected for practical comfort rather than high fashion. Not having the faintest idea of what might constitute appropriate wear on a tiger hunt, but recalling Gareth's pointed remarks at the Herbert party about items of female apparel cluttering up the jungle, Melissa had dressed as inconspicuously as possible. Nevertheless, the spectacular impact that Maree Chandler was making, made her feel positively dowdy!

'Oh dear,' breathed Melissa, frowning. 'I do hope Mrs Chandler is not on our elephant! You *are* riding with me, are you not, Stephanie?'

Stephanie looked momentarily flustered, then coloured a bright pink. 'No . . . well, as a matter of fact . . . Nigel . . . er . . . Mr Bannister has asked me . . .' she stopped, covered in confusion.

Melissa looked at her and smiled, giving her a reassuring hug, as her eyes twinkled. 'Never you mind,' she said with understanding, 'I shall be quite all right even if . . . if Mrs Chandler is to be my riding companion.'

'Oh? I was hoping to grab that privilege for myself, Miss Castlewood!'

Melissa turned around with a start as her heart took a flying leap into her mouth. Gareth Caldwell had appeared out of nowhere at her elbow and was watching her with humorous eyes as a faint smile played on his lips. She flushed, her sudden pleasure making her stiff and formal.

'As you wish,' she said coolly, very annoyed at her

reaction to his presence. She cast a surreptitious glance up at the verandah where Maree Chandler was casting baleful glances at her. Gareth followed her gaze and laughed, ignoring the incensed Maree.

'Don't *you* wish?' he asked softly, his eyes a blaze of mischief.

Melissa returned his look with admirable equanimity. 'It matters little to me who is to be my riding companion, as long as he is reasonably adept with a gun.'

'Oh, I think I am *reasonably* adept,' he teased, 'at least I can guarantee you won't be called upon to make an unwilling breakfast for the beast!'

Melissa bit her lip in vexation as she heard Maree Chandler's caustic laugh up in the verandah. She was furious that Gareth should choose to make sport of her in hearing of Mrs Chandler, but before she could think of a suitable retort, Tom Patterson joined them.

'Shall we go, Caldwell?' he asked, looking at his pocket watch, and bowing hurriedly in Melissa's direction, 'the tiger's been spotted in the south heading towards the river.'

Stephanie and Nigel Bannister were already on their elephant and, as everyone else got ready to mount, Maree Chandler strolled down the stairs languidly and appraised Melissa with a cold, supercilious stare. Then turning to Gareth she remarked acidly. 'I thought you would ride with me, Gareth!'

He appeared unfazed by her frontal attack. Peering down the barrel of his rifle, he smiled devastatingly without looking at her. 'My dear Maree,' he said smoothly, 'if I did, I would irrevocably offend Tom who has been waiting in breathless anticipation for the pleasure of your company this morning.'

Taken by surprise, Tom Patterson opened and closed his mouth like a gasping fish, then rallied admirably. 'Of course I have, of course I have,' he said quickly, then winked, 'especially as Millie is safely away in the hills! Shall we?'

Tightening her lips angrily, with a murderous look at Melissa, Maree flounced off with Tom, knowing she had been subtly tricked but unable to do anything about it. Gareth laughed softly at her retreating figure.

Melissa frowned in tart disapproval, successfully concealing her inner jubilation. 'Wouldn't you rather ride with Mrs Chandler?' she asked caustically. 'After all, she is such an *old* friend, isn't she?' She couldn't resist the barb although she felt ashamed of her uncharacteristic cattishness.

'I would,' he replied quite blandly, 'but I can see from your face that you have a great deal to say to me. Rather than have you suffer apoplexy, I've decided to help you get it all off your mind!'

In chill silence, she allowed him to help her on to the back of the elephant. Cheerfully, in complete disregard of her thundery face, he took his place beside her, giving instructions as to how she should sit if she wanted to avoid falling off. She took it all with cold disdain, trying to ignore the fact that, in his sleek, well-fitting dark brown trousers and open necked white cotton shirt, he cut an extremely dashing figure indeed.

Slowly, the elephant lumbered forward, swaying alarmingly. Melissa gasped as she felt herself sliding sideways, but then felt the gentle—and wholly unwarranted!—pressure of his arm around her waist as he steadied her. His nearness was excruciatingly exciting, especially as his hand lingered casually on her waist longer than strictly necessary. She sat for a while in rigid silence, feeling herself melting in the shattering radiance of his charm, and extremely irritated with herself for doing so. Hardening her heart and assuming an expression of cold severity, she said, 'There is a question I would like to ask you.'

'Indeed?' he raised a quizzical eyebrow, his lips curving in a complacent smile. 'I thought there might be!'

She ignored the remark. 'Was it necessary for you to hold up Mr Carstairs' coach the other night? Don't the diamonds you steal from the mines satisfy your avarice?' Two high spots of colour appeared on her cheeks.

'Yes,' he said mildly, 'they do. But then, a little bonus on the side is not to be spurned, now is it? And Fred Carstairs is a pompous old ass who needs taking down a peg or two.'

'Pompous old ass or not,' she said angrily, 'he has arranged for extra troops from Madras to try and catch you.'

'And you are concerned for my safety?' he mocked, 'How touching!'

'I am not the *slightest* bit concerned for your safety,' she retorted, 'but I *am* concerned for my own! Has it occurred to you that, should your hideout be discovered, I shall be in serious trouble with the authorities as well? You have no *right* to endanger my position with all your . . . your *obnoxious* escapades!'

'Had you been so concerned about staying on the right side of the law,' he retorted lightly, 'you would have certainly turned me over to the authorities earlier. But you haven't, now, have you. *Why not?*' His flashing eyes threw her an open challenge. Having no answer to give, she contented herself with an angry toss of the head and looked away pointedly.

Gareth sighed. 'Why is it?' he asked in barely concealed exasperation, 'that whenever we meet, we fight? Can we not declare a truce for the moment? After all,' he surveyed her through half closed eyes, 'we *are* on the same side!'

'Are we?' Her voice was tired and unhappy.

'You *still* don't trust me, do you?'

'I . . . don't know,' she said slowly. 'Sometimes I do and sometimes I can't bring myself to. You are such a . . . a *chameleon*, changing colours to suit the circumstances.'

Gareth threw back his head and laughed. Even Melissa had to smile. 'By gad!' he exclaimed, 'That is the best description I have ever heard of myself—although it wasn't meant to be a compliment, now was it?'

'No,' said Melissa firmly, but unable to keep her lips from twitching with imminent laughter, and annoyed at the same time, 'it was *not!*'

She sniffed and looked away, annoyed that her anger could be dissolved by him with such little effort, but determined not to let him be aware of this. The jungle around them was by now dense and marvellously cooling. The trees were all in full leaf and hosts of brilliantly coloured birds with unfamiliar plumage filled the air with strident cries. Here and there they

caught a glimpse of herds of *cheetal*, the mellow-eyed
spotted deer so abundant in these forests. Somewhere
in the far distance was the muted and monotonous
sound of drums as the beaters came closer and closer,
pushing the tiger towards them. Ahead of them and
behind, the other elephants lumbered with slow
majesty, their passengers watchful and silent.

Gareth sat lazily by Melissa's side but, in spite of his
seeming indolence, his body was taut and his eyes
alert and darting. Melissa felt a surge of excitement
rush through her body as she sensed the urgency in the
air. Although Gareth was holding his rifle with casual
ease, she could see his finger was never far from the
trigger.

They left the dense jungle and emerged into the
open, now surrounded by tall grass. Melissa knew
that this was typical tiger terrain, the slender, down-
tufted grass, sometimes as tall as eight or ten feet,
providing an excellent cover for the feline predators.
In the near distance, she could see the glint of water as
the river approached. Banks of purple, red and white
balsam dotted the banks and presented a delightful
picture. But Melissa was far too occupied to concern
herself much with scenery. The four elephants that
carried their party, separated and fanned out, surrounding a hollow in the river bank. Melissa noticed
that the beaters had fallen silent, and knew it was
because the prey had been sighted close at hand. Her
heart began to thump rapidly against her ribs; it was a
moment of breathtaking suspense.

As she looked around trying to catch a glimpse of
the tiger, Gareth touched her gently on the arm and
pointed towards the hollow. For a moment, she saw

nothing. Then, suddenly, through the tall, feathery grasses, she caught a glimpse of deep yellow. The elephant crawled forward inch by inch, amazingly quietly. Very slowly, Gareth raised his rifle and took aim but he did not fire. She puzzled for a moment, then realised why. The head of the tiger was now quite clear as it drank thirstily from the water in the hollow. Obviously, Gareth did not want to destroy the beautiful head which he would have had to do from his present angle. He waited. The tiger drank his fill, then came forward a little, turning sideways in the process.

Immediately, Gareth's gun roared, followed by two more shots in rapid succession. The tiger sprang into the air with a frightening snarl, then turned towards their elephant and in wounded fury, leapt on to the trunk of the animal! Melissa all but screamed as the elephant reared and slashed the air with its trunk trying to shake the tiger off. The *mahout* slid back and almost fell on top of Melissa and, for a few moments, there was noisy chaos with everyone shouting at the same time. Then, as Gareth positioned himself again, resting the rifle on the terrified *mahout's* shoulder, his gun roared anew. With a final, rending snarl, the tiger shot up into the air and fell back on the ground, thrashing around for a brief moment, then becoming still.

For a split second nobody spoke, then everybody shouted at once. Nimbly, Gareth jumped down into the grass, the rifle still aimed at the supine tiger. Melissa knew the big cats were known to play possum with great skill—as some hunters had learned to their regret. But this time, the tiger was well and truly dead, shot twice, both times through the neck. Closer examination revealed that it was, in fact, a tigress, enormous and quite splendid looking, its jet black stripes standing out in magnificent contrast to its golden fur. For a moment Melissa gazed upon it with sympathy, sorry to see the end of such a majestic creation of Nature.

Gareth looked up briefly and noticed her expression of regret. 'She's done away with eleven adults, two children and countless cattle,' he said dryly. 'I would suggest, if you have any sympathy, keep it for them.'

'Well done, Caldwell,' Tom Patterson said, not without envy. 'From where I was I couldn't get a clear enough shot.'

'I could,' interposed Nigel Bannister wryly, 'but my rifle jammed.'

'It doesn't matter who got her,' said Gareth impatiently, 'the main thing is she's dead and won't terrorise the villages any more.'

By this time a huge crowd had collected around the kill and the beaters, all from the surrounding villages, were jubilant, knowing that they needn't fear any more for their families and their livestock. Very peremptorily, the carcass was loaded on to one of the elephants, and the hunting party started back for the lodge. On the way back, Tom Patterson bagged two *cheetal* for the pot and it was a very happy and lighthearted group that returned to the base camp, well past noon.

There was a great deal of flurry and excited activity back at the lodge, with the dead tigress on prominent display on the front lawn. Melissa noticed that as soon as they dismounted Maree Chandler took charge very determinedly of Gareth, retiring with him into a corner, talking animatedly. Melissa shrugged and turned away from them, not wanting to become an unwelcome third. Pretending uninterest, she made her way to the room allotted to her and Stephanie in the lodge, happy for a chance to wash and freshen up. At the back of the lodge, the servants had already got a roaring fire going and the two *cheetal*, rapidly skinned and disembowelled, were already on the spit being roasted.

Lunch, although very late, was delightfully unusual, consisting of large, juicy chunks of roasted venison and *chappatis*, the flat, unleavened Indian bread brought piping hot, straight from the fire. It was served out in the open, under the spreading *saal* trees and everybody ate out of improvised plates of banana leaves which eliminated any subsequent washing up.

'Well, Miss Castlewood,' laughed Tom Patterson as they relaxed on the grass after lunch, 'it has been an exciting first *shikar* for you, has it not?'

'Indeed it has,' exclaimed Melissa feelingly, 'I thought the tiger—or rather, tigress—was heading straight for me when she attacked the elephant!'

'Oh, you had nothing to worry about,' Tom replied, 'Caldwell here may be a lazy devil, but he certainly knows how to handle a rifle!'

If Gareth Caldwell heard the remark, he made no reaction. Lying flat on his back under a bright orange flame of the forest tree, he was fast asleep. Maree Chandler, never far from him, sat against an adjoining tree trunk reading a book. Throughout the day, she had taken special care to treat Melissa with the utmost disdain, openly chagrined by Gareth's choice of riding partner. Melissa, on her part, was equally anxious not to cross swords with her, knowing Maree to be a woman of unpleasant disposition. However, in spite of her caution, she found she could not avoid her altogether.

It was as they were getting ready to leave later on in the evening, that Gareth strolled up to Melissa and said brusquely, 'I would advise you to discontinue your early morning riding sorties.'

Melissa looked at him surprised. 'Do they really worry you?' she asked with a trace of wistfulness.

'Indeed they do!' he said sharply. 'If you land yourself in a mess, I shall have to do the mopping up—and I have neither the time nor the inclination!' Abruptly, he walked away.

Oh! Melissa clenched her fists in frustrated fury. Why did he have to spoil everything with remarks like that? At times he was really quite intolerable! As it was, she was very put out because he had spent much of the afternoon paying court to the delectable Maree, ignoring her completely. Indeed, Melissa was quite appalled at the turbulence of her own feelings and shocked that the little green demons of jealousy could find so welcome a home in her heart. She realised she was committing a grave folly by falling in love with a man who had scant respect for the law; a man who, so overtly, could be seen to have romantic interests elsewhere. Yet, she could not forget the frightening, *exquisite* passions his touch had produced in her innocent body. He attracted her alarmingly and made the blood pound at her temples with resounding, reverberating force. Oh, how utterly humiliating to be in love with a man who looked upon her as a wayward juvenile and a burden of considerable nuisance value!

It was as Melissa was waiting by her carriage for Stephanie to join her for the journey back, that Maree Chandler walked up to her.

'I see that Gareth and you,' she began imperiously, 'suddenly have a great deal to say to each other?'

Melissa was greatly taken aback, but bristled at the offensive question. Nevertheless, she managed to smile quite sweetly. 'If Mr Caldwell requires anyone's permission to hold a conversation with me, he doesn't seem to be aware of the fact. Perhaps you should inform him accordingly.' She was about to turn her back on Maree and step into her carriage, when the incensed woman placed a firm hand on her arm.

'Gareth Caldwell has broken more hearts than you could ever imagine, Miss Castlewood,' Maree Chandler's eyes glinted dangerously. For a moment, Melissa was reminded of the tigress as she fought for her life clinging to the elephant's trunk. She had no doubt that, threatened, as she felt now, Maree Chandler was as dangerous an adversary as the man-eater! 'If you insist on so flagrantly trying to attract his attentions, you will undoubtedly live to regret it!' With a vicious laugh, Maree Chandler swung on her heel and flounced off haughtily.

Melissa stared after her, speechless. It was a distressing, thoroughly unpleasant incident and she felt furious with Gareth for having made her a butt for Maree Chandler's hostility. As far as she was concerned, they were welcome to each other. How *dare* he involve her in his sordid little peccadillos! Stephanie's arrival with the ever attentive Nigel Bannister put an enforced stop to Melissa's silent ragings and, much dejected, she climbed into the carriage for the journey home.

Back at Koh-i-noor, she found Roy Chandler waiting for her return.

'I just came round, Miss Castlewood,' he said, 'to let you know that Fred Carstairs has issued a permit in your name to visit the diamond mines. Would tomorrow be suitable for you?'

'Oh!' exclaimed Melissa, very pleased. 'Yes indeed. Tomorrow would suit me very well. How kind of you to have taken the trouble to inform me personally!'

Roy bowed formally. 'It is my pleasure, Miss Castlewood. I shall arrange for my coach to pick you up from Koh-i-noor at ten in the morning. It is not a long ride to the mines, but a rather hot and dusty one. You should be able to return by luncheon.'

'Oh, thank you, Mr Chandler,' she said, 'I do look forward to seeing your famous mines and I shall remember your instructions regarding clothing.'

Roy Chandler laughed. 'I was merely having a little joke at your expense, Miss Castlewood. I cannot imagine any circumstance under which you could be suspected of stealing my diamonds!' He threw back his head and roared with laughter, and Melissa had to smile. She again wondered silently how such a very pleasant man could have happened to marry the volatile Maree and, more pertinently, how he could tolerate being cuckolded so blatantly almost under his nose. She felt a surge of anger against the absent Gareth Caldwell. It was quite scandalous! But then, she had also noticed—not without a certain involuntary relief that Maree Chandler's interest in Gareth Caldwell seemed rather more ardent than his in her. That she was besotted with him, there was no doubt. But what about him? Did he reciprocate her feelings? Perhaps not. Perhaps she was reading far too much into his attentions? Men as attractive as Gareth Caldwell inevitably collected women around them. It was possible that for him, this was just another mild flirtation? And perhaps Roy Chandler accepted it as such? Unaccountably Melissa felt much elated at the thought. By the time Roy Chandler left—having mentioned Gareth Caldwell in passing several times without any sign of rancour—Melissa was convinced that this indeed was the state of affairs between Gareth and Maree. It was really quite ridiculous for her to be so agitated by Gareth Caldwell's romantic—or otherwise!—involvements, but she could not deny that the prospect of Gareth exchanging tender caresses with *any* woman, was agonisingly painful to her . . .

Melissa's first glimpse of the famed Altabad diamond mines the next morning, was disappointing. She was not sure what exactly she had expected, but what faced her as she alighted from the carriage, was dreary beyond measure. Noticing her expression of dismay, Roy Chandler laughed.

'Most people come here,' he chuckled, 'expecting a vista of glass show windows with displays of sparkling jewels as to be seen on Bond Street in London! You must remember, Miss Castlewood, that diamonds are extracted from the earth, not in the form of triple-cut brilliants or *en cabochon*, but as rough and very dull-looking pebbles. The cutting which makes them into gems, comes much later.'

Melissa laughed self-consciously at how accurately he had read her reaction. Of course, they had not yet come to where the stones were being mined, but even the exterior of the mine was particularly dismal. The entire area was enclosed by a high wall and, by the side of the solid iron gates, huddled a group of out-houses which were the administrative offices of the mine. In an ante room, all visitors were required to deposit such articles as handbags and scarves. Dutifully, Melissa handed over her own little pochette. The scene beyond the offices was as bleak, being devoid of any vegetation or greenery. Confronting them was a desolate hillock of brown mud and slush. The compound bristled with armed soldiers and sentry boxes with slitted peep holes.

'Diamonds in India,' explained Roy Chandler as they walked up the hillock along a narrow, twisting pathway, 'are found only on the eastern side of the Deccan plateau. The diamond-bearing area, nevertheless, is quite extensive although many mines are now defunct. But it is known that diamonds were mined in this country as far back as the first century AD.'

'This soil appears very strange in colour,' Melissa remarked, 'what is its composition?'

'Well, it's mostly limestone with intermittent clay and sandstone, soil known to be highly diamantiferous. Of course, diamonds are also found in beds of rivers that have passed over such soil.'

They arrived at the crest of the hill and an amazing sight lay spread out before Melissa's eyes. A very deep trough had been cut into the hill at the bottom of which worked hundreds of men. On either side of the trough, on top of the banks, wooden platforms were anchored to the ground. On these platforms enormous metal pulleys with long, thick chains, were bringing up baskets full of what appeared to be rough, brown stones. The baskets were then transported on the heads of more workers to the bottom of the hill where ran a sluggish river.

'These things are *diamonds*?' Melissa asked in disbelief.

'Yes,' Roy chuckled. 'Ugly, aren't they? Who would believe that these wretched, miserable looking stones are what people are ready to destroy each other for!'

'And who would imagine that the fabulous Koh-i-noor was also once as unprepossessing as this!'

'Ah yes,' Roy smiled, 'I can appreciate your special interest in that little bauble since it came from the mines of Kolar not very far from here.'

'But the Koh-i-noor is not the largest diamond to be found here, is it?'

'Oh dear me, no. The Koh-i-noor has historical celebrity but it now has a weight of only 106 and one-sixteenth carats, cut down from the original 186 and one-sixteenth carats. Nor is it, by any means, the most perfect diamond to be found here. The Regent diamond, for instance, is far more valuable, and was originally 410 carats in weight. It has been cut down several times, I'm told, and is now the property of France, but it is valued at about half a million pounds, far more than the Koh-i-noor.'

For a while they stood by the river, watching the diamonds being washed. Roy handed one to Melissa. It was smooth and cold and rather uninteresting, the dull exterior giving no indication of the wealth contained within.

'After washing,' Roy explained, 'the diamonds are weighed and graded and then sent to Madras. India has for many centuries practised the art of gem cutting, but some Europeans prefer to have their stones re-cut once they come into the markets abroad.'

'I remember reading in England about a new diamond mining company in South Africa called De Beers,' Melissa said. 'They seem to be very successful.'

'Oh yes,' agreed Roy, 'De Beers are going from strength to strength I hear. But the South African diamond production is far more than India's, even though it is of more recent origin.'

Melissa was fascinated by what she was learning about the diamond trade. 'But are their stones as large as the ones found here?' she asked.

'I believe so,' Roy said, 'although the first large diamond found there, the Star of South Africa, weighed only 83½ carats. But since then, they seem to have discovered several big stones. In fact, I heard the other day that a diamond of some 457 carats is on its way to Europe from these mines.'

'And the largest found in these parts?'

'Oh, the Great Moghul, definitely. There are disputes about its weight but some put it as high as 280 carats.'

In a large, closely guarded room, the diamonds were being made ready for despatch in small canvas bags sealed down with wax. 'A consignment is due to leave shortly,' Roy said, 'but tight security is of the essence here. For instance, we have to see that the time, the mode and route are a strictly guarded secret. Nobody is allowed to leave the premises until the consignment has left.' He laughed shortly, 'It beats me how this damned rascal manages to get his information! But not for long . . . Mr Sher Singh's goose is about to be well and truly cooked.' His face turned purple with anger.

Hastily, Melissa devised some more questions about the mines to avoid dwelling on a subject that was thoroughly unpalatable to her. Over cups of hot tea they chatted for a while, then Melissa rose to take her leave.

'I am fascinated by everything that I have seen and heard, Mr Chandler,' she said. 'My father used to talk about these mines sometimes and the subject has excited my curiosity ever since. Thank you so much for arranging this visit.'

'I am pleased to have been of service, my dear,' he said gallantly. 'You are lucky indeed not to be tempted by these wicked little stones. Often, they bring nothing but misery.'

'Yes, I know,' said Melissa slowly. After all, it was for diamonds that her Papa had been murdered, just as the lust for them was now driving Chand Ram to seek her own destruction as well.

On the way out, Melissa collected her pochette and climbed into the carriage. With a quick wave of his hand, Roy Chandler disappeared as the horses started up. It was nearly one o'clock and she would soon be home for luncheon. Thoughtfully, she sat back engrossed in silent introspection. It was a pleasant drive back through avenues of coolly spreading mango and casuarina trees and Melissa was lost in idle reverie.

Suddenly, the subdued peace of the afternoon was disturbed with the steady staccato of horses' hooves. The sound came from behind and, as it grew louder, Melissa leaned out curiously to see who it might be.

It was Gareth Caldwell!

'Whoa!' He called out to the coachman, 'Hold on there, will you?'

The carriage pulled up to a halt as his horse came alongside. With a swift move, he dismounted and swung into the seat beside her. Melissa looked at him startled, then pursed her lips.

'Your manner of calling on people becomes more and more unorthodox each day,' she said primly, taking in his dark tan trousers, open necked shirt revealing an intensely masculine chest and wildly blowing dark hair.

He laughed easily. 'I dropped in, so to speak, to collect something you have for me.'

Melissa stared at him, puzzled. 'Something I have for you?'

He pointed to her pochette, 'May I?' Without further ado, he picked it up, opened it and withdrew from inside a small packet. He held it up to her, 'See?'

Melissa's eyes dilated with horror as she recognised what he held in his hand—a white canvas packet from the mines, exactly like the ones she had seen being packed into trunks not a half hour ago!

She recoiled as he tucked the packet securely inside his shirt, as casually as if it were a mere trifle.

'Thank you,' he said politely, 'You have saved me a great deal of unnecessary trouble.' He smiled disarmingly, touched his fingers briefly to his forehead in

a light salute, swung back on to his horse and was
gone!

Melissa stared after him in speechless horror, then
turned and stared at her pochette. How had the
diamonds got into her bag? Who had put them there?
When? The pochette had been in the possession of the
armed guard throughout the time she was in the
mines! Then, as another thought struck her, she
raised her hand slowly and clutched at her throat.
Gareth Caldwell had used *her* to commit another
theft! He had made her an accessory, however unwit-
ting, to a crime! She had been the only visitor at the
site today. Supposing Roy Chandler suspected her
. . . she broke out into a cold sweat at the prospect of
the consequences.

The coachman, sitting above, becoming restless,
coughed. Then, receiving no reply to his discreet
inquiry, he peered inside the carriage anxiously.
White-faced, her eyes wide and unblinking, Melissa
nodded at him absently and the coach started up.

By the time she reached Koh-i-noor, she was con-
sumed by rage. It was unspeakable, *detestable*, that he
should have used her in this manner! How *dare* he
compromise her reputation by involving her in his
sordid affairs! She shivered with fear at the possible
consequences of his action. Would Roy Chandler
connect her with the disappearance of the packet?
Supposing he did . . . ! Supposing he reported his
suspicions to Fred Carstairs? Supposing they *arrested*
her . . . ?

Melissa wrung her hands in utter despair, so devoured with fury at the absent Gareth Caldwell that
she could not even bear to eat a morsel of food

throughout the day. It was obvious, he had an accomplice inside the mines. Who? She tried to think of any suspicious persons she may have come across, but it was hopeless. There had been hundreds of people about, soldiers, officers and workers. It could have been any one of them. *Oh Gareth*, she moaned in silent agony, *how could you have done this to me*?

She spent a horribly restless night, her mind spewing bizarre fantasies, convulsed with fears. When she rose with the first light, her eyes circled with tell-tale black rings, she felt even more fatigued than she had before she went to sleep. As she sat up in bed listlessly, her eyes caught sight of something lying half tucked beneath her pillow. It was a single red rose with a note attached. It read, simply, *Trust me*!

She buried her face in her hands and burst into tears. What an incomprehensible man he was! At least he owed her some explanation for yesterday, some words of advice, guidance. How unfair he was to expect total trust from her when she knew so little of what was happening around them.

The long cry helped to release much of the pent-up tensions of the night and Melissa dried her eyes eventually, feeling better. Over an early breakfast on the terrace, she mulled over yesterday's events. In spite of his totally unpredictable behaviour, she could not help feeling that Gareth Caldwell was, indeed, on her side. She looked at the single rose on the table and her heart softened again. Maybe there was some rational explanation for it all . . . Maybe Gareth knew what he was doing . . .

It was all rather small comfort and her mind was anything but reassured when she set out for her daily ride on Roshni. Half way down the drive, Mohan Das caught up with her as he faithfully made ready to follow her on the excursion, and handed her an envelope. It had been delivered earlier in the morning by an aide to the Prime Minister. With sinking heart, Melissa opened the letter and read it at a glance. 'My dear Miss Castlewood,' she read, 'I shall be honoured if you would dine with me on Saturday at eight. My carriage will call for you at seven. With kind regards and in anticipation, yours very sincerely, Chand Ram.'

The message helped to depress her and excite her at the same time. Would she be doing right in accepting Chand Ram's invitation for dinner? If she did, Gareth Caldwell would be furious. But if she didn't, she might miss a golden opportunity to improve her acquaintance with the enemy! In any case, one thing was certain—she would be quite safe from harm until Saturday!

She turned to Mohan Das observing her silently and said, 'I do not think it is necessary for you to accompany me this morning, Mohan Das. I shall not venture far.'

Mohan Das paused hesitantly, frowning. 'It might be un . . .' he started to say but Melissa cut him off with an impatient gesture.

'I shall be perfectly all right,' she said rather sharply, 'and I know you have other matters to attend to.' Without giving him a chance to reply, she nudged Roshni and cantered off in a mood of irritability.

The freshly fragrant morning air did much to restore her good humour as she flew down the road to the forest. The sun was not yet high enough to make it uncomfortably warm and, it was impossible to remain dejected amidst the colourful tranquillity of nature. Her spirits began to rise again as she galloped on, her thoughts becoming more and more pleasant.

Lost in the mellow warmth of the morning sun and the extensive calm of the countryside, Melissa did not pay much heed to the direction in which she was going. Suddenly she noticed that they were skirting a small but very delightful lake, shimmering gently in the bright sunlight. On a hillock ahead, stood a temple, its dome in silhouette against the blue sky. It was a pretty view and Melissa realised she had not been this way before. She remembered with a feeling of guilt, her remark to Mohan Das about not venturing far this morning. But nevertheless, she decided to explore the little temple, so far from anywhere. Perhaps she could sit and make a pastel of it to send to Mr Winterton. She had been in the habit of carrying her drawing materials with her on her morning rides, for many were the pretty scenes that presented themselves to her on her explorations. She could think of no better way to describe her environment to her friends at home than to send sketches to England with her letters.

Gently, she urged Roshni up the slope and discovered, as she reached the peak, that the temple was in ruins. The walls were cracked and crumbling with patches of moss and climbing weeds. Nevertheless, it presented an attractive view and she decided to spend a few moments making a quick sketch which she could complete on a subsequent visit.

As she walked round the temple trying to find the most suitable viewpoint from which to sketch, she suddenly heard the sounds of human voices wafting gently upwards from the far side of the hill. Curiously, she strolled over presuming that the voices were those of farmers hard at work in their fields below. One side of the hill dropped down steeply into the valley. She peered down from the edge. Not very far below was a wide shelf upon which stood two men, partially obscured by an intervening bush. A sudden gust of wind moved the bush aside for a moment—and Melissa froze in her steps.

The two men on the ledge, involved in deep conversation, were Chand Ram—and Gareth Caldwell!

Unable to believe the evidence of her eyes, Melissa pressed herself into the long grass and slid forward on her stomach, hardly daring to breathe. Chand Ram and *Gareth Caldwell*? The conversation was now louder as she strained to listen, devoured with uneasy curiosity.

'No, I have not changed my mind,' Chand Ram was saying, '. . . I . . . delay matters a little . . .' The occasional gusts of strong wind were scattering the words now and then.

'You still . . . me to proceed?' Gareth was saying, '. . . as planned?'

'Certainly . . . not until . . . little fun.'

Then, Gareth spoke, very clearly, 'Oh, I understand. Your Excellency has taken a fancy to the girl, is that it?'

Chand Ram laughed. '. . . a tasty morsel, wouldn't you say?'

She saw Gareth shrug indifferently, '. . . but not my type.'

'Is that so? You prefer . . . more aggressive . . .

like, er, the . . . Mrs Chandler, eh Caldwell?' Chand
Ram laughed again very loudly this time and slapped
his thigh.

'When . . . want it done?'

'Soon, soon . . . not getting cold feet, Caldwell?'

Gareth's response came through with complete
clarity as the wind dropped. 'No, Your Excellency,'
he said dryly, 'For a half share in Koh-i-noor, I would
cheerfully murder my own mother, let alone the
Castlewood girl.'

'. . . extraordinary man, Caldwell! That is why . . .
good partners. And now . . . business. The consignment?'

Melissa saw Gareth hand him something which
Chand Ram put inside his jacket pocket.

'. . . cash payment only,' Gareth said coldly.

Chand Ram shook his head, but withdrew a packet
from his inside pocket and handed it to Gareth. '. . .
hard bargain . . .'

Gareth opened the packet and said something
indistinguishable. Chand Ram again shook his
head. Much of the argument, obviously about money,
was lost in the wind but finally, Gareth Caldwell
shrugged, tucked the envelope inside his shirt and
laughed.

'. . . have to pay and pay well . . . Sher Singh's
services . . .'

As Chand Ram put a friendly arm on Gareth's
shoulders, the two men turned and walked away,
their voices fading.

Melissa put her head down in the tall grass and lay
stunned. Even with the few phrases she had managed
to catch, the full import of the conversation was

unmistakable. Chand Ram and Gareth Caldwell were partners in crime.

And, for a price, Gareth Caldwell had undertaken to kill her!

Paralysed with shock, Melissa closed her eyes as she felt her world slipping away from under her feet. Gareth Caldwell was going to kill her! It was incredible, unbelievable but . . . she could hardly mistrust the evidence of her own eyes and ears. The man she considered her friend, the man she had grown to *love*, was nothing more than a paid assassin!

For an interminable while she lay in the grass, sick with misery, numb and uncaring. Then she rose, too miserable even to cry, and slowly made her way back home. She went straight up to her room, locked the door and lay down on the bed, eyes closed in anguish. How stupid she had been! What an utter *fool* to be taken in by superficial charm and a glib tongue! How Gareth Caldwell must despise her for the easy conquest he had made!

Unable to face the world, she informed Zarina that she did not feel well and intended to sleep through the day. And then, finally, the tears came, bitter and abundant. She had never felt so utterly wretched in all her life.

CHAPTER
SEVEN

How long Melissa slept she did not know. But when she finally awoke, still tired and drained, the sun was low on the western horizon and the shadows had lengthened considerably. Weary, utterly dejected, she lay still for a while, re-living the nightmare scene of the morning. In the brief space of less than half an hour it seemed that her whole world had come crashing down around her ears. The pain in her heart was almost unbearable. Oh, how she hated Gareth Caldwell for having caused it!

Slowly, she rose from her bed, her body aching, her eyes red and swollen. She called for Zarina, waiting patiently outside the bedroom door for her mistress to rise.

'I would like some very hot tea, please Zarina,' Melissa said.

Zarina looked at her anxiously, then stretched out her hand and felt Melissa's forehead. She started.

'Madam very hot,' she said worriedly, 'Madam has fever. I call Dr Herbert *sahib*.'

'No, no,' said Melissa sharply. Then, ashamed of her unnecessary brusqueness, she smiled. 'I shall be all right by the morning, Zarina. I have merely caught a slight chill during my ride this morning.'

I cannot face anyone, Melissa thought miserably, at

least not yet. I must be alone for a while. As Zarina rushed off to bring her some tea, she went into the bathroom and splashed cold water over her flushed face and aching eyes. Her head hurt terribly. All she wanted to do was to crawl back into bed and be left alone with her thoughts. The wash helped to clear some of the cobwebs from her mind and she sat in bed and sipped the steaming tea gratefully. The plate of food that Zarina had brought for her, she felt she could not face and pushed it away.

'At this moment, Zarina, the sight of food will make me sick. Please take it away. I promise I shall eat in the morning.'

Reluctantly, Zarina removed the plate but hovered around watching with anxious eyes. 'I call Mohan Das?' she asked.

'No,' said Melissa hastily. 'It is not necessary. There is no reason for alarm. I shall be perfectly well by the morning, I promise you. If I need anything during the night, I will call for you. Goodnight.'

Firmly, she closed the door behind Zarina. The last person she wanted informed of her indisposition was Mohan Das. He would undoubtedly report to Gareth Caldwell—who might well call upon her again in his usual insolent manner. She could not bear the thought of seeing Gareth again. At least, not yet! She first had to regain control of her shattered senses. It would be disastrous and so demeaning to let him see her like this. She could already hear his smooth phrases of hypocritical sympathy, his pretended anxiety. The very thought of it made her nauseous. What a fool she had been, what an unutterable fool!

But, she said to herself, wiping away renewed tears

and getting up to sit by the window, she must not allow herself to go to pieces merely because of silly sentiment. There was still a job of work to be done. She still had to do everything within her power to foil this devilish partnership between Gareth Caldwell and her father's murderer. How cleverly Gareth had strung her along, giving her just enough information to make her trust him. The man was a ruthless thief and a potential murderer to boot. Goodness knew how many other crimes he had committed as well. They were both busy defrauding the British government of the diamonds—and she was *still* allowing Caldwell to use her house as his headquarters!

Cold fingers climbed up her spine when she thought of just how easily Gareth could climb into her room and do away with her without batting an eyelid. How naive she had been to continue letting him use his den at Koh-i-noor! Obviously, she could not allow the situation to continue unchanged. But who could she turn to for help in Altabad? She went through the list of people she had met since she had arrived. Of course! Fred Carstairs, the British Resident! He had offered her his help should she ever need it. He was an officer of Her Majesty's Government—obviously, he was the person to whom she must now turn. Without a moment to lose!

Quickly, she sat down at her desk and composed a careful letter to Fred Carstairs. 'Dear Mr Carstairs,' she wrote, 'Once you had very kindly offered me your help should I ever need it. I now find there is a matter of great urgency on which I need your advice. I would be extremely grateful if you could kindly make it convenient to call on me at Koh-i-noor sometime this morning. Yours sincerely, Melissa Castlewood.'

Putting the letter in an envelope, she sealed it carefully with gum. Then, she paused. To whom could she entrust the task of delivering the letter to Mr Carstairs? Mohan Das was, of course, out of the question and she knew that many of the other servants were involved with Gareth Caldwell's nefarious activities. Suddenly, she remembered Hafiz. Dear, kind old Hafiz, so loyal to the memory of her father! Quickly, she called out for Zarina, who came running, and asked her to fetch Hafiz from his quarters. When he arrived a few minutes later, slowly shuffling into the room, she said to him casually, 'Oh, Hafiz, Mr Carstairs has very kindly offered me some plants from his garden. I wonder if you can think of someone trustworthy who can take this note to his house?'

Hafiz thought for a moment, then said, 'Mohan Das, he take?'

Melissa forced herself to laugh lightly. 'I do not want to disturb Mohan Das now that the stables are being cleaned out. I was wondering if one of your sons could possibly take it down for me?'

Hafiz nodded. 'My son going Altabad early morning. He take.' Melissa handed him the letter. Something in her eyes did not escape the old man. He stared at her for a moment, then said quietly, 'My son, he take note. Tell nobody. You trust.'

Melissa heaved a sigh, grateful for the few words of immediate understanding. She took his hand in hers.

'You are my friend, Hafiz,' she said, touched, 'I shall depend on your discretion.'

Even though the fever still raged, she felt much lighter in heart. I must not let myself go to pieces, she told herself sternly. I shall not think any more of Mr Caldwell. Tomorrow, I shall confess the entire situation to Mr Carstairs. He will know what to do and will undoubtedly help me.

Nevertheless, she slept badly that night, frightening nightmares chasing each other through her fevered mind. She was standing by a cliff with Gareth Caldwell. He put his arms around her and she was happy. Suddenly, his face changed from that of a friend to that of a horrible monster. She felt his hands tighten around her neck as he pushed and pushed. She felt herself falling, falling, falling . . .

She awoke with a start, bathed in cold sweat, shivering. She pulled her bedclothes tightly around her, terrified. The sweat had broken the fever but she felt weak and giddy headed in its aftermath. She rose, bathed her face and neck in cold water, then lay down again. Finally, exhaustion overtook her again and she lapsed into the merciful oblivion of a dreamless slumber.

When she awoke again, the fever had left her completely although her legs still felt unsteady. It was late in the morning, almost nine o'clock. With a start she remembered her note to Fred Carstairs. He might be arriving any moment! Hastily she rose, washed and changed and called for Zarina to bring her some breakfast. As soon as she saw the food tray, she realised just how hungry she was. She ate ravenously, feeling much better afterwards in body and in spirit. Mr Carstairs had not arrived yet. Perhaps he was busy and would not be able to get away until later this morning.

However, it was almost noon before Hafiz came up

bearing a note in his hand. It was the same note she had sent Fred Carstairs. The Resident was not in town and would be away for another two days!

Melissa went cold with disappointment. Again, fear coursed through her veins. Her only chance of help, gone! Now there was nobody she could turn to. The Herberts were dear, dear people but could hardly be expected to be of assistance in a matter as delicate as this. In any case, Celia was an inveterate gossip and the last thing Melissa wanted was for the whole of Altabad to learn what was going on at Koh-i-noor!

And then, like a flash, she remembered her dear friends, Anne and John Morrison. Only last week she had received a letter from them, full of kind concern. They had repeated their invitation to come and stay. Apart from that, John Morrison was a seasoned Government officer with more than a casual idea of Altabad affairs. The thought of having to expose Gareth Caldwell was still, strangely, a painful one. However much she may wish to deceive herself, she was deeply in love with him. But, she decided, hardening her heart, she could no longer condone his evil doings merely because of her own silly weakness. It was the most agonising decision she had ever been called upon to make in her life—but now her duty was clear. She must not flinch!

I must send them a message immediately, she thought. But with whom? And what could she say in a brief message that would convey to them the seriousness of the entire situation? They would sense her panic and would panic themselves, becoming, perhaps, indiscreet in the process. No, there was only one course of action open to her. She must go to

Metapilly herself! But how? She could not take her newly acquired coach without everyone knowing where she was going and, somehow or the other, Gareth Caldwell and Mohan Das would undoubtedly smell a rat and try to stop her.

Roshni! She would *ride* to Metapilly on Roshni, alone and secretly! Metapilly was only fifty miles away. If she started out soon after dark, she would arrive early in the morning. Then she would be safe, safe in the hands of the kindly Morrisons. Oh, how she longed suddenly for a sight of their open, friendly faces and the sound of their gentle voices . . .

Through the afternoon, she laid her plans carefully, waiting impatiently for dusk to fall. Knowing that Gareth had spies everywhere, she gave no outward indication of anxiety, carrying on with her duties around the house with nonchalance. She dreaded the thought of Gareth suddenly appearing in her room, but she hoped that nothing would precipitate such a visit. In the early evening, she thought up an errand for Mohan Das and despatched him to the Herberts in town. He would be away for several hours . . .

As dusk began to gather, the clear, blue sky of the day darkened ominously. This was the season of sudden storms, she knew, hoping that it wouldn't rain. But, soon there was thunder to be heard and occasional flashes of lightning appeared, streaking across the black skies threateningly. By eight o'clock, the first drops of rain began to splatter, soon giving way to a steady downpour. Normally, Melissa would have been delighted at the prospect of a heavy shower for the garden, but tonight her heart sank. What if the rain continued throughout the night?

Nevertheless, praying for the storm to pass soon, she carried on with her preparations, packing a light bag with her immediate requirements. Then she summoned Zarina.

'I am still rather tired, Zarina,' she said, yawning. 'I think I shall have an early supper and retire for the night. I intend to take a sleeping draught before I go to bed so I do not wish to be disturbed. I shall call you when I waken in the morning.'

After a light supper, she went into her room and locked the door securely. She sat down to write a note to Zarina. Her absence was bound to be noticed sometime in the morning and she did not want there to be any panic. In the note, she informed Zarina that she had decided to visit the Morrisons in Metapilly for a few days and they were not to worry. The change would do her good. Of course, there would be bewilderment at the strange manner in which she had crept away, but that could not be helped. By the time Gareth Caldwell heard of her departure, she would be in safe hands and by the time she returned, Gareth Caldwell would be equally safely behind bars!

She propped the envelope up against her pillow so that Zarina would not miss seeing it in the morning. The rain still beat down mercilessly against the window panes and the sky was jet black. She changed into warm clothing and put on a pair of thick, walking boots. Then, there was nothing to do but wait.

It was well past ten o'clock by the time the storm had spent its fury and subsided into a light drizzle, although the wind still blew hard. The thick pall of black clouds was beginning to part and here and there was an occasional patch of moonlight as the moon struggled valiantly through. Melissa quickly extinguished her lamp and opened the bedroom door. Outside, all was quiet. She knew Zarina slept at the far end of the sitting-room and would, by now, be deep in slumber. Softly she opened the sitting room door, paused a moment, then, bag in hand, tiptoed down the stairs. There was no one about. She knew that there were guards posted here and there and Caldwell had eyes and ears everywhere! But tonight was the night of a Hindu festival and she could hear strains of songs from the servants' quarters. Undoubtedly—and hopefully!—all the staff would be involved in merrymaking.

Keeping close to the walls of the house, she crept towards the stables where Roshni was tethered. Surprised by her unexpected night visitor, the mare neighed once or twice as Melissa approached, but she put her hand gently on the horse's nose and stroked it. Immediately, as if sensing her mistake, Roshni fell silent. Quickly, Melissa strapped the saddle on to her back. Then, reins in hand, she led Roshni towards the gate. She knew there was a path through the jungle that was a short cut to the main road. But she also knew that it was a path used frequently by Caldwell and his men. There was no other way to the main road except up the main drive. Fortunately, the night was still pitch black, the moon having lost its battle against the storm clouds, and she managed to pass down the drive in peace, her heart beating like the drums she could still hear faintly from the servants' quarters.

It was not until she reached the main road that, with a sigh of relief, Melissa mounted the horse. The road before her was clear bathed in very pale, occasional moonlight. Until the clouds blew away, she had to proceed slowly and very carefully. The dark forest on either side of the road was grim and silent. But Melissa was not afraid. She had traversed this road every morning on her solitary rides and knew it well. She knew that the creatures of the forests were far more honourable than human beings. They would watch her silently and maybe wonder, but they would not attack unless threatened.

She could not travel fast as the road, after the heavy rain, was soft and slippery. Here and there, rivulets ran across the path, making the going even slower. She had to wait until the moon appeared in full force to be really sure of where she was going. Another danger was the fear of landslides from the hills on either side of the road. She could hear the silence of night being shattered every now and then with a heavy fall of stones and rocks.

The centre of the road was higher than the sides, and firmer, so Melissa kept to the middle, going as fast as she dared. The recently softened surface of the road also deadened the sound of Roshni's hooves for which she was grateful. As they progressed, the road became drier and Melissa nudged Roshni gently with her stirrups. Immediately, the mare broke out into a dutiful trot and the going became faster. The night was still dark but Melissa could tarry no longer. She had to reach Metapilly before dawn broke and it was already, she guessed, well past midnight.

Suddenly, in the far distance behind her, she heard an unfamiliar sound. She paused, briefly, and listened, her mind fully alert. Then she recognised the sound—and her heart froze. It was the sound of hoofs. Somebody was coming up behind her!

With a gasp, chill icicles running up and down her spine, she broke into a gallop but was again forced to slow down as Roshni stumbled over a large pothole in the road and almost sent her flying from the saddle. Fearfully, with her heart in her mouth, she looked around. She could see barely anything; it was still very dark. On one side loomed the jungle, unfamiliar and forbidding. On the other, the steep hillside, black and wet, formed an insuperable barrier. The sound of the hooves was now clearer—and closer!

Quickly, Melissa dismounted. She grabbed the reins and led Roshni down towards the jungle, climbing off the road into a large, muddy ditch by the side of the road. Her breath was coming in short, frightened gasps. She did not know who could be abroad on so vile a night—certainly no one with good intentions!

Sending Roshni into the trees with a gentle pat on her flank, Melissa crouched down in the ditch, keeping her head low down, her face almost scraping the side. The ditch was full of muddy water but she did not notice. Her only hope of escaping detection was to remain very still in the pitch blackness. Maybe the rider, whoever he was, would pass by without noticing them. She closed her eyes in silent prayer and stuffed a corner of her cape into her mouth to deaden the sound of her harsh breathing.

The rider was now very close indeed. In the darkness, he too was proceeding with care. She heard the hooves pass by slowly, not five feet from where she crouched. Then, just as he rode past, the clouds broke suddenly and the light of the moon illuminated the countryside. *Oh God*, breathed Melissa agonisingly, *let him not see me!*

But almost immediately, the hooves came to a halt. She sensed the rider dismount and she heard his heavy boots squelch in the mud. *Merciful heavens, he has seen me, he knows!* The heavy footsteps came closer and closer, then stopped not more than a foot away from the top of her head. She heard a match being struck and found herself bathed in a yellow glow. With a strangled gasp she looked up—straight into the stormy face of Gareth Caldwell!

For a moment there was a stunned silence as they stared at each other, she in total terror, he in grim bewilderment. He spoke first. 'I followed you from Koh-i-noor. Where the hell do you think you're going?'

Melissa continued to stare at him, with shock and fear. He kneeled down and with one hand, grabbed her roughly and pulled her on to the road.

'Are you quite mad?' he asked furiously through clenched teeth. 'Is there not a single grain of intelligence in your head?'

His face was like black thunder. The very sight of his expression petrified her even further. She stumbled against a stone and as he put out a hand to steady her, she found her voice and suddenly screamed, 'Don't you dare touch me or I'll . . .'

'What the . . .' with a furious oath, he clamped his hand across her mouth. She began to struggle. He was going to kill her now! With one arm he held her in an iron grip, the hand still firmly across her face. With the other hand, he swiftly removed his scarf and tied it around her mouth. In the pale moonlight, her eyes were wild and staring. Grabbing her around the waist, he flung her on to the back of his horse, holding her legs against the sides firmly. Melissa struggled desperately, kicking out in all directions as much as she could, her arms flailing helplessly. Ignoring her struggles, cursing and swearing, he swung himself into the saddle, holding her down like a bundle, then whistled for Roshni.

Almost fainting with shock, Melissa felt her mind go numb. They began to climb, where to she did not know. On the steep, slippery hillside, the horse stumbled and slithered dangerously and yet they kept going higher and higher. All at once, she stopped struggling. Her head fell limply down and her arms and legs went still. It was the end, she knew, the end . . .

Suddenly, they stopped and Gareth pulled her roughly down on to the ground.

'Look!' he shouted, 'Look *there*, you little fool!'

Weakly, Melissa opened her eyes as her ears filled with a fearsome, thunderous roar. Underneath her, the entire hill began to quake and rumble. The moonlight was now bright and clear as she turned to look in the direction in which he was pointing. Immediately, Melissa's eyes widened in utter amazement. Just ahead, the entire hillside seemed to be pouring down like a waterfall—and crashing on to the road below, the road on which they had just been. Had they still been there, they would have been crushed to death in the thunderous landslide!

She stared at the horrific sight, speechless and stunned, then turned slowly to look at Gareth Caldwell.

His face was like murder, his eyes inflamed with fury.

'The next time you decide to kill yourself,' he raged, 'I will let you go to hell. I am sick and tired of playing nursemaid and I am sick and tired of your stubborn whims and fancies!'

Melissa closed her eyes as she felt a faintness creep all over her. Slowly, she sank to the ground and sat down with her head on her knees.

'Why should you care,' she asked wearily, 'It would only make your job easier if I *did* die, wouldn't it? And you would still get your half share of Koh-i-noor!' She buried her face in her hands and burst into tears.

Gareth Caldwell's mouth fell open in blank astonishment. For a moment he said nothing too amazed to speak. Then, slowly, he sat down on a rock next to her.

'Would you mind telling me,' he asked very deliberately, 'what the devil you are talking about? Or is it part of the same madness that brings you out in the middle of the night for a spot of riding practice?'

Melissa raised her tear stained face and looked at him bleakly. 'Don't try and pretend any more,' she sobbed, 'I have found out everything. Chand Ram has hired you to k-kill me in exchange for my house, hasn't he? I know all about it, so don't bother to lie to me now, you . . . you double-faced, lying, d-deceitful . . .'

Unable to go on, she choked and again buried her face in her hands, sobbing hysterically. 'Well, now is your ch-chance . . . k-kill me and be d-done with it . . . no one will ever know . . .'

For a moment, Gareth Caldwell remained absolutely still, not saying a word. He waited patiently until her sobs subsided. Then, he pulled out his handkerchief and handed it to her.

'Wipe your face,' he said abruptly, 'You have mud all over it. In fact, you look quite a sight.'

Silently, Melissa took the handkerchief, wiped her face carefully, then blew her nose into it very loudly, dabbing her eyes dry. Then, unable to contain herself any longer, she poured forth the entire story of how she had overheard the conversation between him and Chand Ram near the ruined temple on the hill by the lake. She left out nothing, the words stumbling out one after the other.

'Kill me if you have to,' she ended bitterly, no longer caring, 'Kill me now! I no longer wish to stand in your way of half share of Koh-i-noor!'

Gareth listened to her without interruption, without contradiction.

'All right,' he said suddenly as she finished, 'How would you like to die? I owe you at least that!'

Melissa gasped. 'You mean you *are* going to kill me now?'

Gareth pondered. 'I don't know. Let me think for a moment. Chand Ram wants you alive at least until after the little rendezvous over the intimate supper. Isn't that what he said? I should hate to deprive him of his pleasure.'

Melissa stared at him in horror. Oh, what a villain incarnate the man was! Her eyes again filled with bitter tears.

'For goodness sakes, don't start howling again!' he ordered brusquely. 'Don't you think it's been wet enough for one night?'

Suddenly, she flared up, her temper exploding. 'Oh, if only I were a man,' she stormed, 'I would thrash the living *daylights* out of you!'

He laughed. 'And if only I weren't a gentleman,' he said, 'I would spank you from here into next week!'

'*Oh!*' She stared at him furiously, her fists clenched into tight, angry balls.

Suddenly, he sighed very deeply and shook his head from side to side. 'Melissa Castlewood,' he said in a voice of utter despair, '*What* am I going to do with you?'

It was not the reaction she had expected. Defiance, more lies, smooth talk, perhaps. But this . . .

'Wh . . . what do you mean?' she stammered. 'Do you deny that such a conversation did take place between you and Chand Ram?'

'No,' he said mildly, 'Since you heard most of it with clarity, I can hardly deny it.'

'Are you and Chand Ram not partners in crime?'

'Yes,' he admitted again, 'I fear that we are.'

'You steal the diamonds belonging to the British Government to give to him, *sell* to him?'

'I do, although the price often leaves much to be desired!'

'And he knows that you are Sher Singh?'

'Certainly he does! You silly little birdbrain, how could I carry on my night profession without his help?'

'And . . . and you have promised to kill me on his orders?'

'Yes,' said Gareth totally unperturbed, 'I have promised him your pretty little head on a plate for a half share in Koh-i-noor. It is quite a prize, after all, you must admit.'

Tears welled up again in Melissa's eyes. 'You admit everything, *everything*!'

'Why not, since you are not going to live to tell anyone!'

'Oh, Gareth,' she cried in anguish, 'How could you, how *could* you—after all the *lies* you told me!'

'They are not lies,' said Gareth quietly. 'Every word I have told you is the truth!'

She gaped at him, mouth open, uncomprehendingly.

He laughed softly, throwing her his scarf. 'Your face is still disgustingly dirty! Unless you wipe it, I refuse to kiss you.'

CHAPTER
EIGHT

IT WAS only after Gareth Caldwell had taken her in his arms and kissed her very thoroughly, many times over, that the time finally came for the long overdue explanations. Melissa's head was reeling under the onslaught of his lips, refusing her any coherent thought at all. Breathless and dizzy, she put her head against his chest and pushed him away.

'You have a great deal of explaining to do, Gareth Caldwell,' she gasped.

'Indeed I do,' he said releasing her finally, 'even though you are the most stubborn, wilful and *silly* girl I have ever known! Did you really believe that I would kill you?'

'What do you expect?' asked Melissa accusingly, 'I *still* don't know what the truth is!'

Gareth sighed as he sat down on a rock and motioned her to do the same. 'You yourself once said that, in order to destroy an enemy, one must get to know him first?'

Melissa nodded.

'It has taken me months of hard work, not always pleasant, to work my way into Chand Ram's confidence. To do this, I have had to show *proof* that I am his brother in crime. After all, he's no fool, and persuading him to become a partner was not easy, I can tell you that.'

'And whose side *are* you on, Gareth?' Melissa asked, her eyes still suspicious.

Gareth grinned. 'On my own,' he said softly. 'I have my personal axes to grind. What Chand Ram wants more than anything else, is—Koh-i-noor.'

'But you delivered to him the packet of diamonds as well!'

'He needs money to finance his own little intrigues *until* he gets Koh-i-noor.'

'And you used me to do it!' Melissa glared at him angrily.

'It was the only way,' he said blithely, 'I could get them in a hurry. Don't you see, Melissa,' his voice was impatient, '*he now thinks of me as a friend!* By promising to send you packing, I have not only convinced him further, but also safeguarded you from *his* hired henchmen. Can't you see the advantage of that, for goodness sakes?'

'Yes,' said Melissa slowly, 'I can.' Suddenly she smiled, her eyes clearing. Gareth Caldwell had not deceived her after all—he *was* a friend. Maybe even more!

And he had kissed her *again*!

'You had no right to make me suffer the way you did,' she said severely. 'I very nearly went right out of my mind with agony.'

He leaned over and kissed her very lightly on the nose. 'Do you trust me now?'

She pondered the question, then nodded imperceptibly.

'You don't seem very sure!'

Melissa bit her lip. 'I'm not sure about *anything* as far as you are concerned! You're so . . . so *unpredictable*!'

He laughed under his breath. 'How dull it must be to be always predictable! And talking about unpredictability . . . would you have really given me up to the authorities in Metapilly?'

'Yes,' she said coolly, 'Of course I would have! You *deserved* to be taught a sound lesson for leading me up the garden path like you have.'

'If you *had* reached Metapilly,' he said quite seriously, 'you would have done incalculable harm to . . . many people, most of all to yourself.'

'You *still* talk in riddles,' Melissa cried in exasperation, 'You have no right to keep me in ignorance of the truth!'

'If we are to work together, Melissa,' Gareth explained patiently, 'we must trust each other implicity. Is that understood?'

'Yes, but . . . I will *not* be made an accomplice in your . . . your activities! Is *that* understood? What if Roy Chandler does begin to suspect me? What do I do then?' She again found her agitation mounting.

'He won't,' said Gareth confidently. 'There is nothing to connect you with the theft. Take my word for it.'

Melissa sighed. 'I have taken your word for so many things,' she said, 'I'm sure I don't know why!'

'It's because,' he said standing up and brushing down his trousers, 'you find me totally irresistible!'

Melissa gasped. 'What an unbearably arrogant man you are!' she cried as the colour rushed to her face.

'There are times, I assure you, when I find you very *resistible* indeed—unlike, of course, your . . . your Maree Chandler!' The words tumbled out before she could stop them.

Gareth's eyes widened in surprise. 'Maree Chandler? What has Maree Chandler got to do with us?'

'Not with us,' said Melissa nastily, unable to help herself, 'with *you*!'

Gareth tilted his head to one side and observed her through narrowed eyes. 'Little girls like you,' he said caustically, 'should not put their noses into matters that do not concern them! Maree Chandler is very . . . useful to me, one way or another.'

'Useful?'

Gareth lifted a finger warningly. 'I don't owe you any more explanations than I have already given you. So, no more questions please, there's a good girl, because I will not answer them.'

He was treating her like a wayward child again! 'Oh, you're impossible!' she burst out, stamping her foot angrily.

'Not at all,' he said, his expression deceptively mild, 'When you get to know me better, you will find I'm very possible indeed!'

In spite of her temper, Melissa burst out laughing. It was so difficult to remain angry with him!

'That's better,' he said, 'And now, I don't know about you, but I'm exhausted after this absurd wild goose chase across the country.'

'It's so . . . pleasant out here,' said Melissa wistfully, reluctant for the magic moments to end.

'Well then, *you* stay on,' he said briskly, 'I want to go back and get some sleep.' But his eyes were twinkling irrepressibly. He held out a hand and pulled her to her feet.

They rode back mostly in silence, but it was a silence filled, for Melissa, with a very deep contentment. Her heart soared with rapture as she smiled to herself in the dark, re-tasting every one of the kisses he had showered on her face. Her body felt light and languorous, aching with the beginnings of a strange desire.

The rain had stopped and the moon was now out in all its glory. The night was wonderfully cool and the breezes laden with the smells of wet earth. She was almost sorry when the journey came to an end.

'I will have to leave you here,' he said as they approached a closely-knit thicket.

'Is this where the tunnel emerges?' Melissa asked curiously.

'Yes. As you can see, it is very well concealed and we have made it even more so.'

'Surely, you don't . . . *live* in the hideout?' she asked. 'I heard someone say you have a bungalow on the far side of town.'

Gareth's eyes twinkled. 'Certainly. I have a very fine establishment as befits an English gentleman of wealth and leisure. We have to keep our horses *somewhere*. If you are really a good girl and do exactly as I say, one day I shall invite you to tea and give you real English marmalade.'

'And what would your Maree Chandler say to *that*?' Melissa asked mischievously but with a sharp edge to her voice which she could not repress.

'We will ask Maree Chandler as well. Then you can both fight it out over the muffins!' He bent his head

swiftly and kissed her on the lips, lingering a while.
'You don't have to worry about Maree Chandler,' he
whispered, 'or anyone else.'

She put her arms around his neck with a cry and
returned his kiss with so much passion that, after a
moment, he made to release himself gently.

'There are many things I would like to say, Melissa,' his voice was low and husky, 'but not here. There
will be time . . . later.'

Very reluctantly, she let her arms drop. 'How were
you planning to kill me?' she asked, frowning.

'The choice is yours,' he said seriously, 'I could
pickle you in a bath of acid or feed you to the tigers.'

'Ugh!' she shuddered. 'I am rather relieved, Gareth
Caldwell, that we are on the same side. I should hate
to have you as an enemy!'

He laughed and swung himself back on to his horse.
'The next time you do something foolish,' was his
parting remark, 'I *will* put you across my knee and
spank you!'

She reached Koh-i-noor just in time before the first
light of dawn was beginning to stain the eastern
horizon. The house was still deep in slumber as she
quietly tethered Roshni back in the stables. Lightly,
she ran up the stairs, her heart singing silent paeans of
joy. She paused before the mirror in her room and
even in the half light, she looked dreadful! Her hair
hung down in damp tangles and her clothes were
fearfully muddy as, indeed, was her face. But it was
the face Gareth had kissed and all the mud in the
world could not hide its radiance at the moment. How
different was her mood now compared to when she
had left this very room a few hours ago!

She removed all her clothes, gave herself a thorough rub down and slipped into her night dress. Just as the first light of morning struggled against the window pane, she fell wearily to sleep.

It may have been Melissa's imagination, but through the next two days, it seemed to her that the sun was shining more brightly, the birds were singing sweeter and the flowers were blossoming with even more radiance. Indeed, the whole world seemed to be on the verge of bursting into song. She took to working in the garden every morning, humming to herself and smiling secretly.

The hours were speeding by on winged feet. Every night she waited in an agony of expectation for Gareth to visit her in her room, but he did not come. There were times when the knowledge that he was a criminal wanted by the Police, caused her deep anxiety, but only because she feared for him. She had long since abandoned all calls of conscience, swamped by her love for him. How radically her values had changed since she had left England! What would, she thought, Mrs Rutherford have had to say about it all? And Basil Smithers? She had frequent attacks of giggles as she visualised their shocked, horrified faces—'In love with a *bandit*, Melissa?' Mrs Rutherford would thunder, 'Have you taken *all* leave of your *senses*?' On the other hand, Basil Smithers would perhaps merely lift his eyes to Heaven in gratitude for having Saved him from a Woman of Such Low Moral Calibre!

As the week wore on and Saturday loomed ahead, Melissa began to feel increasingly nervous about her forthcoming dinner engagement with Chand Ram.

Gareth had angrily forbidden her to accept the invitation but had not repeated his objection the last time they had met on the abortive journey to Metapilly. Should she go—or make an excuse, as she was sorely tempted to?

Finally, on Friday afternoon, when there was still no sign of Gareth Caldwell, she scribbled a hasty note to him, *Must see you tonight*. According to an instruction he had once given her, she wandered out casually into the garden and, making sure she was not observed, quickly slipped the note into the bole of a *gulmohar* tree at the far end.

After dinner she waited in her room, having dismissed Zarina and with her door securely bolted. Had Gareth received her note? Supposing he was not in Altabad? She had no idea of his comings and goings but she knew he travelled far and wide performing goodness knew what deeds.

Tired of sitting up for him, she put her head down on her desk and, without intending to, dropped off to sleep. When she opened her eyes an hour or so later, Gareth Caldwell was reclining on the settee, his feet stretched out comfortably and his arms crossed behind his head. Melissa blinked her eyes rapidly to clear away the sleep and sat up immediately.

'I . . . I didn't hear you come in . . .'

'I would have been most disappointed if you had,' he said with a bland smile, 'I specialise in soundless breaking and entering—or didn't you know?'

'Yes,' she said dryly, 'I do know.'

'What seems to be the problem? Has anything happened?'

'N-no . . .' she said slowly, 'but tomorrow is Saturday . . .'

'Have you accepted the invitation?' He asked sharply.

'Well . . . I have not refused it . . .'

'In that case,' he said peremptorily, 'I suggest you do, the first thing in the morning. You can think of an apt excuse. Women are good at that sort of thing.'

His expectation of total obedience from her, irked her considerably. 'But perhaps we could use the evening to our advantage, Gareth.'

He glared at her ferociously. 'The boot, my dear child, will be on the other foot! Chand Ram will spin circles around you before you know what is happening. Besides, he may . . . misbehave. I absolutely *forbid* it!'

'*Forbid* it?' she exclaimed with asperity, 'Just because he finds me a "tasty morsel"?'

Gareth flushed. 'If he lays a finger on you, I shall be forced to kill him—and that could ruin everything.'

Melissa smiled, enjoying Gareth's show of petty jealousy, 'You don't think I can look after myself when confronted with an amorous gentleman?'

His face darkened. 'No,' he said curtly, 'You're not the type. You would probably go to pieces and dissolve in tears, like you did the other night.'

Melissa's eyes glinted. 'Oh, really? And who *would* be the type in your opinion—not Maree Chandler by any chance?'

'As a matter of fact, now that you mention it,' he said coldly, 'Yes. Maree can *certainly* look after herself.'

Melissa banged her fist on the desk angrily. 'I will

not be treated like a six-year-old,' she fumed. 'If I choose to go to dinner with Chand Ram, I *will*, so *there*!'

'Very well,' said Gareth furiously, rising from the settee and striding towards the window, 'But if you get into trouble again, don't expect me to bail you out this time. I have far more important matters to see to.'

Without even a backward glance, he swung on to the parapet outside and was gone.

Melissa sat down again heavily, her momentary anger evaporating in dismay. *Why* does he always bring out the worst in me, she wailed inwardly. And now, I am truly on the horns of a dilemma. I wish I knew what to do! But on reflection, his visit had not been a complete failure. Gareth Caldwell was violently jealous! Well, it served him right, she thought smugly. Maree Chandler indeed!

The next morning, Saturday, in spite of an invigorating ride in an entirely new direction, Melissa's nervousness returned in double measure. Would she be able to manage Chand Ram if he made any attempt to . . . molest her? She certainly did not lack courage, but he would not require much strength to overpower her. She would, after all, be completely at his mercy. The thought made her more and more agitated. If only Gareth could advise her, promise to be somewhere on hand, tell her what to do . . .

Just as she had made up her mind to send a note of regret to Chand Ram immediately on her return to Koh-i-noor, Gareth Caldwell appeared behind her, galloping up at high speed along the river. He signalled that she should follow him up a far hill, then cantered on ahead. Wonderingly, but much relieved, she followed, debating the possible cause of the unexpected encounter. Half way up the hill, he suddenly disappeared from view within the hill side. When she arrived a few moments later at the place, she noticed the opening to a deserted cave inside which he had dismounted. Looking around curiously, she followed suit.

'Another of Sher Singh's hideouts?' she enquired coldly, still much put out by his behaviour last night.

'Yes,' he said shortly, 'but let us not discuss that for the moment.'

'Well, what is it that you wish to discuss—having dragged me all the way up here.'

'I didn't drag you, as you put it! As far as I can see, you trotted along quite willingly. But . . .' he held up a hand, '. . . I don't have time to bicker today.' Something in his tone stopped Melissa from a cutting retort. He walked over to the mouth of the cave and stood staring out with his back towards her.

'I have had second thoughts about your dinner engagement with Chand Ram.'

'Oh?' she asked sharply, memory of their argument not forgotten.

'In fact,' he said, turning to face her, 'You may be right. Your presence in Chand Ram's apartments could be quite . . . useful.'

'Oh?' She was surprised at his volte-face.

'Yes. In fact, *very* useful. So, I have decided to help you on condition that you help me.'

'How?' Melissa was extremely intrigued.

'Chand Ram has a safe in his bedroom concealed behind the wood panelling. This is where he keeps his cache of diamonds and several documents which I have no doubt are extremely incriminating.'

'How can you be so sure?' she asked.

'I *am* sure,' he said irritably, as Melissa listened with growing unease. 'In any case, that is not the point. The point is . . .' he paused.

'What has all this to do with *my* dinner engagement?' Melissa asked, suspiciously.

He smiled the devastating smile he knew would forgive him anything. 'With your help,' he said mildly, 'I intend to burgle Chand Ram's safe tonight.'

'What!' Melissa gaped at him incredulously, then burst out laughing. 'Surely, you cannot be serious, Gareth Caldwell!'

'Oh, I am,' he asserted, quite in earnest. 'I suggest it purely as a business arrangement. I will see to your protection, if you help me get the keys to that safe.'

'I shall do no such thing!' she cried, outraged, 'How *dare* you even suggest it!'

'In that case,' said Gareth rising, 'You can go into the lion's den alone. I wash my hands of the entire affair.' He made a move towards his steed.

'No, wait, Gareth,' she said hastily, appalled at the prospect of having to deal with Chand Ram on her own. 'It's . . . it's not a fair proposition! It's . . . it's nothing but *blackmail*! I . . . I wouldn't know what to do, where to start. Why, I've never stolen anything from anyone in my life before!' She was almost in tears at his utter callousness.

He surveyed her quite calmly, his eyes hard and unrelenting. 'It is no better than what Chand Ram deserves,' he said ruthlessly.

'But . . . he has already paid you for the diamonds, has he not?'

'Not enough,' said Gareth curtly. 'It could hardly be called a fair deal.'

'B-but if you d-double cross him, he will certainly kill you!'

'That,' he said lightly, 'is my problem. Yours is to get me the keys.'

Melissa shook her head miserably. 'I will not be able to do it, Gareth. I shall . . . die of fear!'

'What has happened to the courage, the indomitable spirit of the Castlewoods,' he scoffed. 'Have you forgotten so soon that he killed your father?'

'No,' she whispered brokenly. 'I have not. But . . .' She looked at him in abject misery and, all of a sudden, she was in his arms.

'You can do it, my darling,' he breathed, kissing her ear with infinite tenderness, his hand caressing her hair. 'It's very important that you do . . . *for me*.' He kissed her on the lips, his hands cupping her face gently. For a moment she stood still, eyes closed, savouring once again the exquisite closeness of his body against hers, all her resistance melting like wax around a flame.

'If you do this for me,' he said softly, '*once*, Sher Singh will be laid to rest forever.'

Her heart leaped, 'You mean it?'

'Cross my heart and hope to die,' he said quite seriously.

'You are asking me to become a member of your gang for one night?'

'Exactly!'

Melissa rested her forehead against his chest for a moment. Before her eyes, again, flashed a vision of Mrs Rutherford and Basil Smithers, as *she* reached out for her smelling salts and *he* for his Bible! She giggled.

'You find the idea amusing?' he asked, surprised and pleased.

'I find the idea *outrageous*,' she said severely, unable to keep her eyes from twinkling, 'but . . . when you kiss me, all reason seems to vanish unaccountably!' He kissed her again, hard and long.

'You may be a saucy wench, but you certainly are going to be the prettiest member of Sher Singh's gang!'

'What if I get . . . caught?' she asked, paling at the unsavoury prospect.

'You will not get caught,' said Gareth heaving a vast sigh of relief. 'Now, listen carefully, this is what I want you to do . . .'

CHAPTER
NINE

THAT evening, Melissa dressed with more care than she had ever done for any occasion in her life. It was a perilous adventure she was embarking on and nothing must go wrong. In spite of her qualms, she seemed to be gripped by a strange excitement, all reason in her mind laid to rest by her passionate love for Gareth Caldwell. Whether he loved her in return or not, she was far too confused to know. It was enough that he had held her in his arms, kissed her with a passion matching her own, caressed her with hands of loving tenderness . . .

After some thought, she had selected a stunning outfit of pale lemon organza which she had bought in a mood of extravagance in London from a very exclusive dressmaker. It had cost more than she had ever dreamed any dress in the world could cost. But she had not been able to resist the light, fluffy confection, so unlike the hand me downs she had worn all her life. She knew the dress suited her well, bringing out the deep, bronze lights in her hair, now brushed to silken perfection. She decided that for once, perhaps, she needed a touch of colour in her cheeks and added a discreet patina of red. In her hair, which she had decided to wear loose except for a tortoise-shell comb at the top, Zarina placed a single marigold. Her large eyes she lined with a fine line of black to bring out the smoky depths of the deep, deep blue. Examining herself critically in the mirror, she knew she looked remarkably alluring. If Chand Ram was to be seduced—however briefly—every one of her charms must be brought into play. The evening was important to Gareth—that was all that really mattered. And she knew he would not let her down. He would be there, somewhere, guarding her, watching over her every move. The thought filled her with reassurance. For tonight, she was as much an outlaw as he!

On to her wrist, she slipped a small, yellow satin pochette. She felt it again to make sure it contained what it should—a neat, pearl-handled pistol that Gareth had given her this morning. She had never touched a pistol in all her life, much less had occasion to fire one.

'Keep it,' Gareth had said, after a few quick lessons in its use, 'but for goodness sakes don't use it unless you absolutely have to. It wouldn't do to blow out either my brains or your own by accident!'

'I'm sure I'm not as bad as all that,' she had exclaimed, aiming at the target Gareth had set up on a tree and managing to hit it four times out of ten. She could tell he had been reasonably impressed.

'I can see we'll make a full fledged bandit out of you yet,' he had teased, grinning.

Feeling the hard outlines of the pistol reposing quietly within her handkerchief in her pochette now, she felt adrenalin course through her veins with renewed force. She wondered—had her darling Papa been alive, what would he have had to say now? But in some very mysterious way, she felt instinctively that her Papa would have approved, why she could not tell.

'You will take care, Melissa, won't you?' Gareth had asked her for the hundredth time this morning. 'Don't take any chances with Chand Ram. I know him—he has eyes in the back of his head! If anything goes wrong, make an excuse—anything—and *leave*. Will you promise me that?'

'Yes,' she had promised solemnly, 'And I will be very careful, Gareth. I will try to do exactly what you want.'

For an all too brief moment he had held her close and kissed her on the lips, dissolving all her fears in a magic instant. 'There is a great deal at stake, Melissa. Perhaps more than you know.'

They had left it at that.

Chand Ram's carriage was announced promptly at seven. With a final few minutes in which to revise Gareth's instructions and with a last look in the mirror, Melissa walked down the stairs, her head held high, her poise perfect. She spent the journey in silent contemplation of the evening ahead, the hollowness in the pit of her stomach increasing as the Palace drew nearer, but there was little she could do about it except pray that all went according to plan. There was no withdrawing now!

Chand Ram himself was waiting for her at the Palace entrance. As the carriage pulled up in the porch, he personally opened the door and extended his hand to help her alight. He bowed, then raised her hand to her lips. Melissa shuddered involuntarily, then smiled and made a casual remark about the weather.

'My dear Miss Castlewood—Melissa,' Chand Ram exclaimed, 'You look ravishing this evening. I shall have great difficulty in keeping my eyes off you!'

Melissa lowered her lashes and fluttered them modestly. 'You flatter me, Your Excellency,' she cooed, 'surely I am not deserving of such high praise.'

Chand Ram laughed delightedly as he escorted her up the stairs. 'Beauty and modesty are rare bedfellows indeed! But I am even more enchanted by your manner than with your singular loveliness! Come, my dear, let us sit down and become better acquainted than we are at the moment.'

The apartment tonight seemed even more opulent than previously. All the chandeliers had been lit, making the room sparkle with illuminations—a fact that relieved Melissa greatly. Another reassuring factor was that the apartment bustled with many sided activity. In one corner sat two musicians, one with a *sitar* and the other with a pair of drums, making soft music. Melissa was only just beginning to acquire a taste for the melancholy strains of Indian music and the sound, she had to admit, was very pleasant without being obtrusive. Once again her eyes wandered around the room, dazzled by its almost oppressive flamboyance.

'You approve of my humble abode?' Chand Ram asked with such patently false modesty, that Melissa could not hide a smile.

'It is . . . beautiful,' she said, her voice awe struck with just the right amount of admiration. 'Your Excellency is obviously a gentleman of fine taste.'

Chand Ram's chest expanded visibly as he accepted the compliment with a slight tilt of his head. He pulled himself up to his full height. 'Allow me to offer you a glass of my best sherry, imported from the finest cellars of Spain. You did mention that you are very partial to sherry, did you not?'

'Indeed!' said Melissa, her eyes shining with anticipation, 'I would be most pleased to accept.'

Chand Ram clapped his hands twice and a splendid, uniformed valet appeared from behind a curtained doorway. He gave the order in brisk Hindustani, adding some comments that Melissa could not understand. She observed him closely as he conversed with the servant. He was again dressed in an immaculate, well starched white uniform, his chest covered with medals and decorations. Her eyes stole down to his belt on which, to one side, dangled a chain attached to two large brass keys. Hastily, she averted her eyes in case he noticed her glance, but her hand crept surreptitiously behind her back towards her pochette. Together with the pistol, Gareth had given her two replicas of the brass keys on Chand Ram's belt! She hoped it would not be too difficult to make the substitution when the time came.

'Ah!' exclaimed Melissa springing up from the sofa quickly as Chand Ram sat down again next to her alarmingly close, 'What a delightful balcony!' She walked towards it rapidly, immediately followed by Chand Ram.

'This balcony faces east,' he said, 'That is considered to be extremely lucky by my astrologers.'

'Oh, how very interesting,' said Melissa, leaning forward on the railing, 'Does Your Excellency believe in astrology?'

'Of course,' he said, surprised at the question, 'It is

all written in the stars, my dear Melissa. In India we place great importance on the position of the planets. They control all our destinies.'

'I know very little about astrology,' Melissa said, smiling naively, 'Perhaps Your Excellency would be kind enough to enlighten me?'

They were interrupted briefly by the valet who placed the two glasses of sherry carefully on a table. Chand Ram offered her one and took the other himself. He raised his own glass above his head and asked, 'Shall we drink a toast to the chaste memory of your dear father?' Then, without waiting for an answer, he added, 'To Colonel Guy Castlewood, a true friend of Altabad.' With one gulp he emptied his glass and immediately poured himself another from the bottle on the table.

Melissa lowered her eyes to hide the look of disgust that leapt into them, and sipped delicately. Chand Ram raised his glass again and murmured softly, 'To a . . . better acquaintance?' He paused and smiled meaningfully. Melissa coloured as she read the message in his sharp, beady eyes and quickly averted her head with an embarrassed smile, taking another sip from her glass. Chand Ram laughed under his breath. The valet came into the balcony and said a few soft words to him.

'Excuse me,' Chand Ram said with a sigh, 'I have a small matter of business to attend to.'

As soon as he left the balcony, Melissa peered anxiously around the dark gardens below. Here and there torches flared casting pools of dancing light on the grass, but the darkness was thick all around. Somewhere, somewhere among those trees was

Gareth . . . Her appearance on the well lit balcony, as per his instructions, was to let him know that she had arrived, so that he could time his activity. Her heart thumped wildly within her breast. Was Gareth there at his post? Were all his men as carefully positioned as he had said they would be? He was to give a brief signal with the striking of a match as soon as he had seen her on the balcony. In vain she searched for it. Then, just as she observed Chand Ram make his way back across the room, she saw the split second flame behind a cluster of trees to the right. It was so quick that she was not even sure that she had seen it. Nevertheless, she heaved a sigh of relief and almost fainted with sheer thankfulness.

Turning to Chand Ram quickly, in case he noticed the direction of her glance, she said, 'I see that Your Excellency likes to be surrounded by greenery. You have beautiful plants on your balcony.'

'Yes, I enjoy growing things,' he said, 'and so do you, from what I hear. Your gardens at Koh-i-noor, they tell me, are already transformed.'

'Perhaps Your Excellency will be kind enough to arrange for me to take some cuttings from your Palace gardens?'

'Certainly, my dear. My gardens are at your disposal and I shall instruct the gardeners accordingly. You like my rare specimen of cactus?' he asked as he saw her gaze rest on a plant in the corner.'

'It is most . . . unusual,' said Melissa moving closer to the large brass pot at the far end of the balcony in which rested a plant of very strange, long leaves.

'This cactus,' Chand Ram explained proudly, 'is an unusual breed known as Morning Glory. It blossoms

once every twelve years and the flower of pure white,
is a delight to watch. Alas, it only lasts a few hours,
opening after midnight and dropping before the first
light of the sun in the morning.'

'How extraordinary!' exclaimed Melissa, genuinely
interested in the curious plant. Little did Chand Ram
know the part his Morning Glory was to play in the
evening's events!

'Come, my dear,' he said finally, placing a hand on
her arm, 'let us sit inside where we can be comfortable
and . . . private. I see you have hardly touched your
drink! Perhaps the sherry is not to your liking?'
Before Melissa could protest, he had clapped his
hands and placed an order in Hindustani which Melissa could not follow.

'I myself much prefer my special wine—perhaps
that would appeal to your palate more.'

'I am afraid I am not much of a drinking companion, Your Excellency,' Melissa said with a little laugh
as she settled down on the sofa, reclining in such a
manner that Chand Ram was forced to take the
adjoining chair.

'The man is a heavy drinker,' Gareth had warned
'be careful not to try and match him drink for drink. In
fact, avoid the wine altogether. It is very strong and I
don't especially fancy having to carry you home!'

The valet arrived bearing a salver with two beautiful golden goblets. Chand Ram offered her one courteously, gulping thirstily from his own. Remembering
Gareth's remark, Melissa sipped carefully at the
wine, making sure that it no more than touched her
lips. Even so, she could feel the fire in her mouth and
was grateful for the words of warning.

'You were about to lighten my ignorance about astrology,' said Melissa eagerly, 'I know so very little about such a profound subject.'

Launched on a topic about which he had strong feelings, Chand Ram had a great deal to say over the next hour or so. Relaxed by repeated goblets of the wine, he leaned back comfortably, gradually becoming more and more expansive under Melissa's expert manipulations. Ensuring that his glass was never empty, she plied him with questions, her eyes wide and admiring, her concentration complete. Or so it appeared to him. In actual fact, she barely listened, her eyes stealing every now and then to her watch wondering how long it would take for him to show signs of inebriation. Every time Chand Ram insisted that her own glass should be refreshed, she made some pretext of emptying the drink into a Chinese ginger jar of exquisite porcelain that stood not far away.

By the time the third bottle had been emptied, Chand Ram's face was flushed and his eyes were beginning to look bloodshot and bleary. He seemed very happy indeed.

Nor could he be blamed. Melissa appeared to be hanging on to his every word, rapt with attention, as he told her all the wonderful things his astrologers had predicted for him in the future. In actual fact, she felt she had never worked quite so hard in all her life! When the subject seemed to be on the verge of exhaustion, she leaned forward and examined with a frown all the medals pinned on to his chest.

'You must be a very brave man indeed, Your Excellency,' she purred, 'to have won so many accolades in your career. *Do* tell me how you managed to conquer so many enemies.'

It was an invitation Chand Ram could not resist, so appealing was the look in Melissa's eyes. 'I have had many enemies in my life,' he sighed, 'but God has been good to me.' He leaned forward and his eyes became luminous with a strange light; his voice changed to a sibilant whisper. 'They will not escape from me now. I shall achieve my goal regardless of their perfidy. It is written in the stars.'

Melissa stared at him for a moment, chilled by the note of warning. What faced her was not the slightly ludicrous countenance of a man on the brink of intoxication, but a mask of such menace that she shivered. It was almost as if he had forgotten her existence as, for an eternal instant, his eyes remained focused in the distance perhaps witnessing some event in the future not visible to her. She shivered again but suddenly, as if by magic, his countenance changed. Gone was the momentary viciousness. He smiled.

'Ah yes,' he said quite casually, unaware of the strange interlude, 'I shall tell you how I won my medals . . .'

Melissa gave a long, shuddering sigh of relief and sat back, again immersed in the lengthy monologue. Covertly, making quite sure that his attention was on other things, she stole a glance at the keys hanging on his belt. They were attached to the chain by the simple expedient of a loop. It would not be difficult to remove them—provided the opportunity presented itself. But how?

She redoubled her efforts to ply him with drink

whenever he paused. He insisted on filling her glass each time he filled his own and Melissa had by now counted seven glasses she had emptied into the Chinese vase! The evening wore on and still Chand Ram talked. The musicians had long since departed as had all the other servants. Or maybe they were concealed discreetly behind the curtains. The salon was deserted except for Chand Ram and herself.

It was not until well after ten o'clock that his speech began to slur appreciably and his head lolled a little. Yet, he was far from being out of his senses. The man had the constitution of an ox! She wondered how on earth she was going to substitute the keys unless she could ensure that he passed out completely.

At ten-thirty, Chand Ram finally clapped his hands and asked for dinner to be served. Immediately, lackeys appeared from everywhere, carrying out his bidding with alacrity. They sat at a round mahogany table, polished like glass, in the adjoining dining room. Countless footmen served a relay of endless dishes as they ate out of gold plates and with silver cutlery. Melissa had never seen such splendour in all her life and, under different circumstances, would have been vastly impressed. The food, which came in an infinite variety, was delicious but she found it difficult to eat with any relish. As it was, she could barely swallow a morsel, picking at the food with only a pretence of enjoyment. Chand Ram, on the other hand, ate with gusto. His appetite was voracious. With each course, he asked for a different wine, insisting that she keep him company. In full view of the servants it was impossible to get rid of the wines, so Melissa pleaded sufficiency, knowing she would

need all her wits about her for the unpleasant time
ahead.

By the time dinner was eventually over, her head
swam with the sound of Chand Ram's incessant voice
and she felt increasingly agitated by what she had to
do now. Grateful that the interminable meal was
finally at an end, Melissa rose from the table and
made her way quickly to the balcony.

'It is such a beautiful night,' she said, 'I would like
to stand here for a while and inhale the sweet perfumes arising from your garden.' She leaned over the
balustrades and breathed in very deeply. It was her
signal to Gareth Caldwell that dinner was over and
that, so far, all was well. Slowly, Chand Ram lumbered after her, now having some difficulty in remaining on his feet. With a loud hiccup, Chand Ram put
his hand around her waist and said thickly, 'Let us go
inside where we can be more . . . intimate.'

Melissa recoiled as she felt his arm on her body, not
only because she found it unbearably distasteful, but
also because she feared that Gareth may notice it and
conclude that she was having trouble in controlling
the man. Deftly, with a light, flirtatious laugh, she
moved away quickly to admire a marble statue on a
pedestal. As Chand Ram turned his back to the
garden in order to follow her, she saw, out of the
corner of her eye, another brief flicker of light among
the trees. Gareth had seen her!

'Yes, *do* let us go inside,' Melissa said, mightily
relieved that Gareth was still keeping watch over her,
'then you can show me those swords you took off the
Pathan tribes in the North West Frontier. I should so
adore to hear all about that.'

'The razor sharp swords,' Gareth had told her, 'hang on the wall of his bedroom. Get him to remove them if you can.'

But suddenly, Chand Ram's mind was very far away indeed, from the North West Frontier tribesmen. He seemed to have realised that enough time had already been wasted that evening without its purpose having been achieved. He sat down heavily on the sofa and pulled her down next to him, stroking her bare arm with his huge hand. All the servants appeared to have left for the night although she knew he had guards posted behind the door and down the corridor. Then, to her dismay, she noticed that the valet still hovered discreetly behind the curtained archway leading to the dining room.

Clenching her teeth, she moved closer to Chand Ram and whispered, 'Would it not be pleasant, Your Excellency, if we were to be left alone, just you and me?'

Chand Ram turned his head with an effort, his bloodshot eyes reluctant to leave her lovely face, and noticed the valet. With a muffled oath he shouted something at the man who immediately bowed and went out of the door, closing it firmly behind him. Now, they *were* alone!

Melissa swallowed hard and closed her eyes, her heart palpitating alarmingly. He lurched unpleasantly close and attempted to kiss her on the mouth. Dodging his move, she slipped out of his hold exclaiming wildly, 'Oh, what a beautiful painting! I had not noticed it before!' She ran to the main door through which the servant had just disappeared and, while pretending to admire a large landscape in oils, stretched out an arm and turned the key in the lock. She fumbled inside her pochette and withdrew a twist of paper that Gareth had given her.

'Empty that into his drink as near midnight as possible,' he had instructed.

'Will it kill him?' she had asked, alarmed.

'Unfortunately not, but it will knock him out for a while.'

Before Chand Ram knew what was happening, she was back in her seat next to him, refilling his glass and keeping up a steady patter of inconsequential nonsense. Had he been sober, Chand Ram would have found her behaviour certainly odd, but in his present state of drunkenness, inflamed with his lust for her, he hardly noticed anything.

She lifted his goblet with the powder safely dissolved in the wine, and held it to his lips. With eyes closed in anticipation of the ecstasy that lay ahead, Chand Ram downed the wine in a single gulp, then heaved himself on to his side and lunged at her again.

'Oh, Your Excellency,' she cried shrilly, 'you must be patient! And you have finished your drink without giving me a chance to have mine!' Quickly, she filled up his glass again, pouring a little for herself as well. Battling for time, she removed the empty bottle from the table and carried it slowly to the far end of the room, depositing it on top of the sideboard. She walked back even more slowly, observing him with anxious eyes.

Chand Ram had laid his head back against the sofa and his eyes were closed. In his hand he held his glass. As she neared the sofa, Melissa pretended to stumble and fell heavily against him, managing to spill much of the bright red wine over his white uniform. He opened his eyes with a startled oath.

'Oh, Your Excellency,' she cried in horror, 'Oh, how stupid, how very stupid of me! Oh, I *am* clumsy and now I have ruined your beautiful white coat! How will you ever forgive me . . . *please* let me clean it for you . . .'

She grabbed a napkin from the table and rubbed the front of his coat hard, spreading the stain even more. He made a drugged effort to rise but she pushed him firmly back into the sofa.

'No, no,' he murmured sleepily, trying to struggle to his feet again, 'I . . . shall . . . change . . .'

'Oh, Your Excellency,' she said pouting, desperation making her voice shrill and unfamiliar to herself, 'I am *so* enjoying your fascinating company . . . I shall take your coat and have it washed in a minute . . . no, no, I *insist* . . . after all, it *was* my fault . . .' Tears of frustration came into her eyes as he continued to resist her efforts to remove his coat. He opened his eyes suddenly and a look of surprise came into them as he saw her tears. He put his arm around her waist, smiled groggily and laid his enormous head on her breast. 'Do not . . . upset yourself . . . I shall . . . remove my coat . . .' His voice was thick and slurred and he could barely keep his eyes open now. Obviously, the drug was taking effect, but it had far from knocked him out cold!

'You were telling me about the time you took the tribesmen single-handed . . .' gasped Melissa, working feverishly at getting his coat off.

'My . . . keys . . .' he mumbled, 'Must have them . . .'

'Yes, of course,' she said soothingly, stroking his brow, 'I have them safe with me, see? Now, you just lie back for a moment while I have this stain cleaned in no time at all . . .'

Suddenly, his head lolled to one side and he closed his eyes with a groan, putting a hand to his brow. Quickly, she whisked the coat on to the balcony, removed the keys from his belt and slipped on the substitutes. Then, she ran to the bottom of the balcony and put his keys into the large brass pot that contained the Morning Glory.

'I need those keys for fifteen minutes,' Gareth had said, 'That is all.'

From a carafe she sprinkled water on the coat front to drench it thoroughly and placed it on the balustrades. Quickly, she extinguished the torch on the wall plunging the balcony into darkness. It was her signal to Gareth that the keys were now where he wanted them.

'Where are you, my dearest?' she heard Chand Ram call out. He was *still* not completely asleep!

'I am coming, Your Excellency,' she called back, 'I have washed your coat and it will be dry soon . . .' She ran back into the room, almost fainting with relief that the job was done.

'My valet,' he muttered, 'no need for you . . .' His head rolled back again. Melissa was already by his side, soothing his brow, stroking his arm, urging him to sleep. It was a quarter past midnight by the ormolu clock. Fifteen minutes! It seemed like an eternity! Her heart in her mouth, she watched Chand Ram toss restlessly, still not completely unconscious, opening his eyes dazedly every now and then and subjecting her to glassy stares. There was an expression in his eyes that she could not fathom, as if, in spite of his drugged state, he was trying to work something out. She remembered that she had not succeeded in getting him to bring the swords out of the bedroom. But, maybe, with luck, it would not matter . . .

'My keys,' he said suddenly, his eyes closed but his voice low and strangely steady. 'Where are my keys?' He made a move to get on his feet. Pretending to be playful, she put a palm against his chest and pushed him back.

'They are on the balcony, quite safe . . . I will fetch them for you . . .' She rushed out and, with trembling fingers, removed his belt from his coat. Would he notice the difference in the keys, similar as they were? With a thumping heart she handed him the belt. Without opening his eyes, Chand Ram ran his fingers over the keys, slowly and lingeringly while Melissa watched, cold with suspense. The tactile examination seemed to satisfy him for he turned his red, glazed eyes towards her and smiled.

'You must . . . forgive me . . .' he mumbled, 'never let them out of . . . my sight . . .' Even though his speech was confused, he seemed in reasonable control of himself. She looked at the clock, hardly daring to breathe. Five minutes to go before Gareth was finished in the bedroom! With a monumental effort, Chand Ram stretched out a hand, grabbed hold of hers and stumblingly rose to his feet. Holding her with a grip that was surprisingly firm, he pulled her up, covering her face with wet, slobbery kisses. A stifled scream rose to her lips but she choked it back, trying to fight him off.

'Come . . . we have wasted enough time . . .' His voice was thick with passion as his hands roved her body freely. She stiffened with incredible revulsion, her throat dry with fear. Where oh where was Gareth? *Oh dear God*, she moaned silently, beating her fists against his chest repeatedly, *don't let Gareth let me down*! Her breath came in shredded gasps as Chand Ram lifted her in his arms like a piece of driftwood, his lethargy forgotten, no sign now of the effects of either the wine or the drug. With one foot, he kicked open the door of the bedroom as she struggled helplessly in his massive grip. And then, unable to control herself, she screamed . . .

Almost immediately, a shot rang out, whistled over their heads and landed on the wall above the bedroom door, shattering into flying smithereens a Chinese plate suspended on the wall. With a startled oath, Chand Ram slackened his hold around her waist and she fell in a heap on the ground.

'Come over here, Melissa!' Her knees went weak with relief as she heard Gareth's command from the far end of the room. 'Raise your hands above your head, Your Excellency, I can see you very clearly indeed, so no tricks!'

Melissa looked round the room as she scrambled to her feet and ran over in the direction of Gareth's voice. He sat crouched on his haunches behind a table, the gun resting on the top and aimed straight at Chand Ram.

'*Caldwell?*' Chand Ram exclaimed in utter astonishment, 'What the hell are you doing here? Have you gone quite mad?'

'Not at all,' replied Gareth calmly, getting to his

feet, the gun still pointing at Chand Ram's head, 'I have never been more sane in all my life. We have some unfinished business to settle.'

Chand Ram laughed, his hands rising above his head. 'Come, come, Caldwell! Surely this is taking a grudge too far? What is it you want—more money?'

'I'm afraid it is quite another matter we have to settle tonight, Your Excellency,' said Gareth regretfully.

'Another matter? I don't understand . . .'

From the table, Gareth held up two small packets similar to the ones Melissa had seen in the mines.

'There is this, of course,' continued Gareth, 'but there are also these . . .' He held aloft a thick envelope containing papers.

Chand Ram's face went white, then flooded with a rich, plum colour. For a moment he said nothing, then whispered, 'How . . . how did you get to my safe . . . ?' His eyes turned slowly towards Melissa and he looked at her with such venom that she shivered involuntarily and moved closer towards Gareth. Chand Ram's face again drained of all colour as he lowered one hand slowly and held his forehead with it. He appeared to sway on his feet for a moment, on the verge of imminent collapse. He clutched his throat and said in a hoarse, barely audible whisper, 'I have to . . . sit . . .' Swaying, eyes closed, he stumbled to the settee almost bent double. Just as it seemed as if he would keel over completely, he suddenly lunged, made a grab for a sword hanging on the wall behind the settee and ducked, all in one single lightning move. It was so fast that Melissa barely saw what happened.

'Gareth, look out . . . ,' she screamed and another bullet whistled out of Gareth's gun but embedded itself harmlessly in the settee. Crawling flat on the ground, dodging behind pieces of furniture with amazing agility, Chand Ram avoided Gareth's ammunition easily. As Gareth leaped on to the table, Chand Ram's sword struck out as swiftly as a cobra and flicked the gun out of Gareth's hand, slashing his arm in the process. Melissa screamed again as blood gushed out of the wound, but Gareth seemed unconcerned as he made a leap towards the bed and wrenched the other sword from off the wall, just as Chand Ram came crashing towards him.

As the two men fought silently and grimly, a thunderous clamour started outside the apartment door, and the kicks of a hundred boots seemed to descend on it.

'*Kholo, kholo*!' shouted a confused jumble of voices, 'Open up or we break the door down!' Chand Ram's guards had arrived in force! *Come on Gareth*, Melissa prayed silently, run, *run*! If they found him here, they would kill him. What they would do to her, she had no time to think about. With Gareth's life hanging in the balance her own safety seemed of little consequence.

She watched in horror as the two men fought on locked in deadly combat. That they were both superb swordsmen, there was no doubt. But Gareth, with his lithe, loose figure, was gaining ground as he hounded Chand Ram relentlessly out into the balcony.

'You will not outlive this . . . this doublecross, Caldwell,' Chand Ram hissed as he fought back desperately, 'and neither will the girl!'

Gareth laughed breathlessly, 'I regret that your days of glory are over, Your Excellency. Judgment day is indeed on hand!' The black sleeve of his shirt was wet with blood, but Gareth seemed almost not to notice it as he fought on with one hand, his teeth clenched in grim concentration. Melissa's blood ran cold as the sound of a fresh voice outside rose above the din of the battered door, its wood on the verge of disintegration.

'Open up,' the voice ordered, 'Open up in the name of Her Majesty the Queen!' It was a voice Melissa had no difficulty in recognising—that of Fred Carstairs, the British Resident.

Oh my God! Frantic fear clutched at her heart, Fred Carstairs! *Gareth must not be found here, he must not!* 'Gareth, *run!*' she pleaded, almost in tears, 'It's Fred Carstairs!'

But Gareth seemed not to hear, too intent on the kill at hand, uncaring about the world outside. His brow was covered in sweat, his eyes like slits of gold. Expertly, parrying Chand Ram's vicious strokes with miraculous speed, he forced him on to the balcony. Having to fight while backing away, Chand Ram was at a disadvantage as he tried to dodge obstacles behind him and unable to take his eyes off his opponent even for an instant. A small stool on the floor caught his ankle at the back and he stumbled. In a flash, Gareth had spun his momentarily wavering sword out of his hand and sent it crashing to the ground.

'Get it, Melissa,' Gareth panted, pinning Chand Ram against the balcony wall. Lifting her skirts, she kicked it as hard as she could, sending it spinning underneath a chair.

'Good girl,' gasped Gareth with a brief smile. 'And now, my friend, *I have you*!' For a split second, Chand Ram stared at him his eyes ablaze with hatred. Then, with a roar of fury, he swung the sword aside with a powerful sweep of his arm and, like an enraged, wild animal, flung himself bodily on Gareth. The momentum of his attack wrenched the sword from Gareth's hand as the two men locked in a murderous embrace, grappling hand to hand. With almost superhuman strength, Chand Ram pushed Gareth back into the room, finally flinging him on to the ground, his hands around Gareth's neck in a stranglehold. With an anguished cry, Melissa ran into the drawing room and grabbed her pochette, withdrawing with shaking fingers, the pistol that Gareth had given her.

The two men were writhing on the ground, Chand Ram's fingers still clenched around Gareth's neck, squeezing with all their monstrous might. It was obvious that, in his weakened state, Gareth would not be able to hold out much longer. Holding the pistol with both hands, still shaking uncontrollably, she closed her eyes and fired at the chandelier, praying she would not miss. She did not! The explosion of shattering glass filled the room as part of the chandelier came crashing down, taking Chand Ram with surprise as he looked up and his fingers loosened. With a lightning move, Gareth rolled aside, bringing up his knees and kicking out at Chand Ram's face with all the strength left in him. The kick caught Chand Ram under the chin and his head snapped back with a sickening crunch as he fell over backwards—and lay still.

With a splintering crash of shattered wood, the door of the apartment burst open.

'*Jump*, Gareth,' Melissa shouted above the din, 'Jump from the balcony . . . I'll hold them off . . .'

But weak from loss of blood, Gareth struggled slowly to his feet, his face contorted with sudden pain as he held his wounded arm and grimaced. She ran to him, just as the bedroom door was flung wide open and Fred Carstairs charged in followed by soldiers— and Tom Patterson, the chief of Police. Melissa shut her eyes tight in anguish. It was all over for Gareth! There was no escape for him now . . .

Quickly the soldiers surrounded Chand Ram as he lay in a heap, groaning, and dragged him unceremoniously into the other room. Fred Carstairs stared from Gareth to Melissa and back again, his eyes wide with astonishment. Then, as Gareth swayed and clutched at the bed-post, Fred Carstairs stretched out a hand to support him.

'Steady on!' said Carstairs, then looked over his shoulder. 'Tom? Captain Caldwell needs to be removed to hospital immediately. See to it, will you?'

'Yes, sir,' said Tom Patterson, signalling to his men.

Gareth Caldwell made an effort to stand up, winced with pain—and saluted.

'The papers,' he whispered unsteadily, 'are all there . . . diamonds . . . on the table . . . packets with markings from the mines . . .' He began to stagger but strong hands took hold of him before he could fall, with Tom Patterson shouting out brisk orders to everybody.

Fred Carstairs thrust out a hand, his face wreathed

in smiles, and patted Gareth on the back. 'Well done, my boy, well done . . .'

Melissa stood watching the incomprehensible scene, all her faculties numbed. Through the door she could see soldiers in British uniforms clamp a pair of handcuffs around Chand Ram's wrists as they lifted him bodily off the ground, still alive.

'He won't be able to wriggle out of this one,' she heard Carstairs tell Tom Patterson, 'the diamonds are clearly stolen property. He'll have a job explaining to a court of law how he happened to have them in his possession, in clear contravention of the Treaty. The documents in the envelope will do the rest . . .' He turned to Melissa, staring at him dumbfounded.

'I am not quite certain, my dear,' he said gently, 'what your particular role has been tonight, but I am aware that it was considerable.' He pointed to the weapon Melissa still clutched in both her hands. 'In any case,' he added kindly, 'I can assure you, you no longer have need of this!'

Melissa stared at the pistol in her hands and, without a word, handed it to him. Then, with a deep sigh, she slid gracefully down on to the carpet in a dead faint . . .

CHAPTER
TEN

WHEN Melissa finally came to, she found herself lying on a soft, comfortable bed, surrounded by anxious faces. Slowly, as the people came into focus, she recognised in their midst, the features of Fred Carstairs and the Palace physician. She frowned, then gave a start, as the extraordinary events of the night flooded into her recollection and she realised that she must still be in the Palace. Weakly, she struggled to sit up.

'I . . . I must have . . . fainted . . .' she began rather unnecessarily, 'How very . . . silly of me . . .' She suddenly noticed Zarina sitting near her pillow with a compress in her hand.

'Madam has bad shock,' Zarina said sternly, 'Madam not move.'

'You will be perfectly all right in a little while,' said the Palace physician, adding to Zarina, 'Please fetch Miss Castlewood a hot cup of tea.'

'Who . . . who are all these people . . . ?' Melissa asked wonderingly. Quietly, Fred Carstairs rose to his feet and, in muted tones, asked for the room to be cleared. Then, when they were alone and the physician had also left, he leaned forward over the bed, his eyes filled with concern.

'You have indeed had a gruelling experience, my

dear. But you must not be alarmed any more. It is all over. Chand Ram,' he added quietly, 'is no longer of any consequence to you.'

'And . . . Gareth . . . ?' she whispered anxiously.

The British Resident smiled briefly. 'Gareth Caldwell is in good hands. Dr Herbert is attending to him now in the hospital. Fortunately, he has only suffered a flesh wound, but he has lost a great deal of blood and has to be under medical treatment for a while. There is, however, nothing to worry about.'

'Oh.' Melissa closed her eyes in relief. Sitting up against the pillows and sipping the hot tea that Zarina handed her, she began to feel better as her head cleared. She smiled a little wanly.

'So much happened all at once,' she said, 'I . . . don't understand anything any more . . .'

Carstairs chuckled. 'I know, my dear, a great many explanations are due to you. And a special apology from me.'

'An apology?'

'I did receive your note the other morning. I opened it carefully, read it and then sealed it down and returned it. You see, I could not possibly accept it since I knew exactly what you wished to communicate to me. It was about Captain Caldwell, was it not?'

'Yes,' admitted Melissa, frowning. 'They said you were out of town . . . ,' she paused as a thought struck her, '*Captain* Caldwell?' She remembered in astonishment, that was how Fred Carstairs had addressed him earlier in Chand Ram's apartment.

'Gareth Caldwell is an officer in the British Army. He has been working under my orders all along.'

Melissa stared. 'But he is Sh . . .' She stopped

herself in time and bit her lip in alarm at her slip.

But Fred Carstairs chuckled again. 'Sher Singh? Yes, we know Gareth is Sher Singh. It was Gareth's own idea and made a very effective cover for his real assignment.' He laughed as he saw Melissa's expression of bewilderment. 'Gareth Caldwell is in Altabad on special duty from headquarters in Calcutta. His brief, which was highly secret, was to see to the safe delivery of the diamonds to Madras—and to destroy Chand Ram, using whatever means he could find.'

Melissa digested this information in silence, unable to grasp all the finer points.

'But then . . . why was Gareth st-stealing the diamonds from the mine?'

'Merely to lull Chand Ram's suspicions and to tempt him into accepting Gareth as a business partner. We had planted an accomplice inside the mines— the same accomplice who . . . er . . . made rather free with your purse during your own visit there.'

Melissa frowned in disapproval, much agitated by all these amazing revelations. 'But then . . . if Gareth . . . er . . . *Captain* Caldwell, was working for you, why did he hold up *your* coach as well?'

'We put up *that* little charade to further establish Gareth's bona fides in Chand Ram's eyes. I am told he was delighted when he heard of my alleged humiliation!' Noticing the increasing displeasure in Melissa's eyes, Carstairs covered her hand with him. 'You must forgive Gareth, my dear, for having misled you all along. It was decided that the less you knew, the better for your safety, and whatever he did was in the noble cause of Queen and country.'

'I see.' Melissa failed to be satisfied with the explanation, much annoyed at the manner in which she had been fooled and fed with a tissue of lies—*even* in the noble cause of Queen and country!

'Tonight's little masquerade was planned to expose the stolen diamonds in Chand Ram's possession—incontrovertible proof of his contempt for the law and for the Treaty with the British. The documents in the envelope that Gareth also recovered, supply all the details we need to build a cast-iron case against him, including . . .' his voice became gentle, '. . . including evidence in black and white of Chand Ram's complicity in your father's murder.'

'He can now be punished for that?' Melissa asked quickly.

'We think so. The papers will be thoroughly examined by our lawyers and used to our full advantage. It is what His Highness has been waiting for. The Maharaja has been adamant that Guy Castlewood's foul murder will be avenged.'

'The Maharaja also knew about all this, did he?' Melissa asked, her heart sinking further.

'Yes,' said the British Resident gently. 'It would not have been possible for the British government to act as they did without the sanction of the Ruler of the State, however weak and powerless.'

Melissa sighed deeply. 'So, everyone appears to have been aware of the truth except . . . me!' She bit her lip in embarrassment.

'This was a man's game,' Fred Carstairs explained hastily and apologetically, 'even though your own role in it has been quite considerable and of vital importance. But women after all,' the eyes of the confirmed bachelor twinkled momentarily, 'tend to react strangely sometimes! Consider how easy it would have been for you to have—quite innocently, of course—blown the lid off everything—as you very nearly did when you set out for Metapilly that night!'

Melissa flushed, realising the truth of what he said. 'Had I been taken into . . . into Captain Caldwell's confidence,' she persisted coldly, 'I would not have betrayed his trust.'

'True, perhaps,' Fred Carstairs sighed, 'but it was Gareth's own decision and I have always trusted his judgment in all matters.'

A new thought occurred to her. 'And, Sher Singh's . . . gang . . . ?'

'All highly trained and trusted soldiers in the British Army. In fact,' he looked a little sheepish, 'except for Hafiz, your gardener, and Zarina, who is from the Palace, the entire staff at Koh-i-noor is on our payroll and has been very carefully selected. Mohan Das is our chief courier for the diamonds. It was his idea to use Koh-i-nor as a base. He was, therefore, most put out when you arrived from England to constitute—quite unknowingly, of course—a threat to their cover.'

Two red, angry spots appeared on Melissa's cheeks as she realised the extent of Gareth Caldwell's subterfuge as far as she was concerned. Noticing her rising anger, the British Resident decided on a hasty change of subject. 'You have my most sincere personal thanks for the part that you played in tonight's events. Without your help it would not have been possible for Gareth to have completed his mission. In addition, you saved his life by firing a very timely shot. And I can assure you . . .' he said earnestly, 'at no time were you in any danger whatsoever. Gareth made sure of that. The Palace had been completely surrounded and Chand Ram's guards neutralised even before you arrived here.'

'But supposing . . .' Melissa's eyes narrowed, 'I had refused Chand Ram's invitation at the last moment—as I had every intention of doing?'

Carstairs coughed and his face became ruddier than usual. 'Gareth assured me that you would not. And, as you know, his persuasive powers are . . . er . . . quite considerable.'

A wave of scarlet swept across Melissa's neck and face as she understood the import of his words. What an impudent, insolent rogue Gareth Caldwell had turned out to be! He had made use of her blatantly for his own purposes, however patriotic they might have been! And she, naive, foolish and stupidly gullible, had let herself become putty in his hands, doing his bidding like a puppet on a string! Was it only to gain his own ends that Gareth had made love to her, kissed her with such passion? It was a shattering thought and she slumped back miserably against her pillow, mortified and desperately humiliated. Maybe Gareth had even described to Fred Carstairs every one of their meetings in vivid detail—possibly put it all down in his reports to Headquarters! The thought made her go cold with misery. She turned her face away from the British Resident and buried it in her pillow.

She heard the chair scrape as Fred Carstairs rose to leave. 'You need to rest, my dear,' he said softly, 'but I would just like to add that . . . Captain Caldwell is not only a very brave, very astute officer, but also . . . a fine gentleman. Goodnight, or rather, good morning, Miss Castlewood. I wish you a speedy recovery.'

For a while after he had gone, Melissa lay still, steeped in wretchedness. The astounding revelations of this morning had replaced the seething excitement of the night before. Silently, with eyes closed, she began to recall everything that Gareth had said to her as he had held her in his arms on so many occasions. She remembered the gentle caresses, the infinitely tender look in his eyes. Had it all been in the pursuit of cold, calculated duty? Could he really have been so callous as to exploit her innermost feelings without even a shade of remorse or scruples? They were all agonising thoughts and Melissa felt her heart contract with pain at the possibility of Gareth's perfidy.

The doors of the room were flung open suddenly and a footman announced sonorously, 'His Highness the Maharaja *sahib* of Altabad.' Shuffling slowly, leaning heavily on his stick, the old man walked into the room and sat down on the edge of Melissa's bed. His face was wreathed in smiles, his eyes bright with unshed tears. He was in a state of great emotion.

'My dearest Missy,' he took her hand in his affectionately, 'I would have come earlier but my rheumatism began to play up with all the excitement so I had to rest awhile. I am only too aware of your terrible experiences of the night and I am thunderstruck at the astonishing courage that you have shown!'

'Thank you, Your Highness,' said Melissa heavily, attempting to force a smile, 'but my own part in the events was . . . incidental. It is to Captain Caldwell that you have to direct your gratitude. His performance was undoubtedly . . . brilliant.'

The Maharaja appeared unaware of her depression, too involved in his own elation to notice the bitterness in her voice. 'Yes, I know, I can never thank Captain Caldwell enough for having rid my state of this . . . this pestilence, and for having brought Guy's murderer to book.' Then, suddenly noticing Melissa's lack of enthusiasm, the smile faded from his face and his eyes became clouded with perplexity. 'You are . . . troubled, my dear, why? Is there anything an old man can do to help?'

Ashamed at her churlishness, Melissa pulled herself together with an effort, even managing an excessively bright smile. 'No, Your Highness, I am not troubled,' she lied, 'I am merely rather . . . tired. But I do share most sincerely in your joy. Perhaps now there *will* be laughter again in Altabad.'

He smiled radiantly, reassured. 'Yes,' he nodded happily, 'I am now in the process of despatching a message to my daughter-in-law informing her of the events and requesting her to return to Altabad with her son—my grandson!' He beamed even as his eyes began to overflow with tears of pure happiness. 'We have indeed been without laughter for too long! I shall be forever in your debt—and that of young Gareth and Mr Carstairs. Today, it is a day of rejoicing for my State and a holiday has been declared for all!'

Melissa longed to get back to her Koh-i-noor so that she could be alone with her thoughts, but the Maharaja would not hear of it.

'You need to rest, my child,' he said, 'and at Koh-i-noor, you will be plagued by visitors, all agog with inquisitive questions. Do you feel up to facing them just yet?'

Melissa sighed as she realised the truth of the

Maharaja's perceptions. She knew the news of last night's events would have already spread over the State like wildfire. Inevitably, her own name would be involved and there would be much rumour and gossip. Gareth was safely away in hospital, heavily guarded and protected from unwelcome visitors. Fred Carstairs was capable of taking care of his own interest, experienced in matters of State and well equipped to take on prying questions. She, on the other hand, was very vulnerable and would be the natural focus of attention for the moment. She knew that not the least of the sensations was the true identity of Sher Singh. The best doctors available were at Gareth's bedside helping to heal his wounds. But . . . who was there to help her heal her own?

Reluctantly, but with practical common sense, Melissa decided to accept the Maharaja's very kind offer of hospitality at least for a few days. A guest suite was made ready for her at the Palace and, together with Zarina, Melissa prepared to spend some time enjoying the solitary security the Palace afforded away from wagging tongues. Visitors who requested to see her were turned away politely by the Maharaja's staff and she was left in peace to spend her time as she wished, grateful that she did not have to face the full onslaught of Altabad society just yet.

Mohan Das came to see her every day with news of Gareth who was progressing well. Secretly, she yearned to be at his bedside, but she was determined not to give in to her feelings again—cause of all her present anguish. She had at least expected a personal note of some sort from Gareth. But the messages he sent through Mohan Das were all verbal and perfunctory. He was still not allowed visitors, she learned from Mohan Das—full of apologies to her but beaming with relief that his own ordeal was over. A team of high powered investigators was on its way to Altabad now to assess the situation and to prepare a case against Chand Ram, safely locked in the local jail. According to Mohan Das, Gareth was to submit a full report to the team and despatches of all sorts were flying fast and furious between Altabad, Madras and Calcutta.

But the prospect of all the excitement outside left Melissa cold, too immersed in her own introspections to care. She spent her days reading to the Maharaja, participating in his new found joy as he awaited the arrival of his grandson, or sitting alone in the gardens, brooding. Everyone's cup seemed to be full, except hers! Even the Maharaja was fully preoccupied with his council of ministers, busy preparing new plans of action for the future of his State, bursting with renewed hope.

A week passed and *still* there was no letter from Gareth. She knew from Mohan Das, who saw him every day, that he was recovering well and was in rare high spirits. It was rumoured that, very soon, Gareth would be summoned to Calcutta together with Fred Carstairs. Since the assignment on which he had been sent to Altabad was now more or less complete, it was also rumoured that Gareth Caldwell would shortly be recalled permanently to Headquarters and perhaps be given another posting elsewhere in the country . . .

And what about Melissa's own future? She spent many long, depressing hours considering that most important question. She came to the gloomy conclusion that she would have to stay on in Koh-i-noor which was, after all, her home. But the prospect of remaining in Altabad after Gareth Caldwell had gone made her feel sick at heart, the taste of India turning to ashes in her mouth. She hoped against hope that Gareth would communicate with her, but there was only silence from him. Bitterly, she was forced to conclude that her fears had been only too correct. Having used her for his own ends, exploited her innocent naivety, he had now dropped her like a hot brick, perhaps even forgotten about her existence, remembering her name only as something to be included in his impending report!

Then one morning, Melissa was astounded, but delighted, to learn that the Morrisons had arrived to visit her at Koh-i-noor. Begging leave from the Maharaja and thanking him for his affectionate hospitality over the past few days, she departed for her home under safe cover of darkness.

Seeing the Morrisons at Koh-i-noor, awaiting her arrival anxiously, Melissa was beside herself with joy. She flung herself impulsively into their arms—and burst into tears. Gentle and understanding as always, they allowed her the luxury of a good cry without interruption. It was only when she finally lay back on her bed, exhausted and drained, that John said, very firmly, 'All right. Now, tell us all about it, dear. We have been worried sick about you.'

Much relieved and lightened by the tears, Melissa plunged into a detailed recital of everything that had happened to her since she had first arrived at Koh-i-noor. Everything, that is, except her painful emotional involvement with Gareth Caldwell. Even to the Morrisons, she could not bear to talk of that.

At the end of her saga, John shook his head in admiring surprise. 'What a dreadful time you must have gone through, my dear. I am so glad that we decided to come. It must have been an unbearable burden for you to carry all alone.'

'We came as soon as we heard the news,' said Anne hugging Melissa in relief. 'But what we heard was all so garbled and confused that we felt we had to hear it from you personally.' She turned to her husband accusingly. 'Now you see, John, how terribly *wrong* you were about young Gareth?'

John Morrison hastily cleared his throat, turning a dull pink with embarrassment. 'There was no way,' he said very stiffly, 'in which I could have been aware of the true state of affairs. But yes, I do admit that . . . I was wrong and quite taken in by Captain Caldwell's . . . er . . . *act*.'

'You were not the only one,' Melissa burst out, then bit her tongue as she realised how shrill her comment must have sounded. Anne looked at her sharply with an eyebrow raised. 'I mean,' Melissa amended hastily, 'everyone in Altabad was deceived as well . . .' Then, anxious not to dwell any longer on what had happened, she offered to show them around Koh-i-noor. 'I have been longing for the day you would come to visit me. Now, let us not waste another moment. There is so much that I would like to show you.'

The rest of the day was spent in pleasant wanderings around the estate. Gradually, under the Morrisons' open approval of the house, Melissa found her good spirits returning as she revelled in their lavish praise of her efforts to rejuvenate the property. In spite of Melissa's entreaties, however, the Morrisons could only stay in Altabad overnight. John was on a tour which could not be interrupted at the moment.

'We shall be back in Metapilly by the end of the week,' Anne said to Melissa as they prepared to depart early the next morning, 'and we should so love to have you with us again. You deserve a holiday after your hair raising experiences and perhaps we could make a trip up to Ootacamund in the Blue Mountains so that you can truly recuperate amidst pleasantly cool surroundings.'

'Yes, do think about it, Melissa,' John urged, 'The change will do you a world of good. After all, there is nothing to keep you here now, is there?'

'No,' Melissa shook her head sorrowfully, 'there is nothing to keep me here now.'

Anne observed her face closely, knowing with a woman's unerring instinct that all was, perhaps, not well yet. But wisely, she held her peace.

'Perhaps I could come to Metapilly next Sunday?' Melissa asked. 'That should give me enough time to settle domestic matters here.'

'Sunday would suit us perfectly, my dear,' Anne said. 'We will expect you for tea.'

Melissa stood in the porch and waved to them until the carriage disappeared from view. Then she walked back slowly to the house. Her choice of Sunday for the departure was more than casual. She knew from Mohan Das that Gareth Caldwell was to be discharged from hospital on Monday. And the last person she had any intention of seeing ever again, was the deceitful, double-faced Captain Caldwell! She had learned in the course of idle conversation with Mohan Das that, since he had been allowed visitors at the hospital. Gareth's most frequent caller had been Maree Chandler. It was galling news and had set the seal on her decision to cast Gareth Caldwell out of her life forever.

The few remaining days of the week passed by in resolving sundry details around the house and in issuing instructions to the staff for duties to be performed while she was away. Since some of her staff had been soldiers in the British army and had by now left under orders, she entrusted Mohan Das—who was to stay until Gareth Caldwell did—with the task of finding replacements. The others, who were not soldiers but who were on Fred Carstairs' payroll, wished to stay on and Melissa was happy to accommodate them. Indeed, there were a million and one things to be settled, including that of 'Sher Singh's' erstwhile hideout which Melissa was anxious to have dismantled and closed as soon as possible. It was all rather painful and although Melissa set about the chores doggedly, her heart was not in them.

On the Friday before she was due to leave for Metapilly, Fred Carstairs called. He enquired courteously about her well being, then surprised her with an astounding question.

'I have been commanded by Headquarters,' he began, 'to ask whether you might consider the sale of Koh-i-noor to the British government. You are, I think, aware of the quite considerable value of your estate?'

Melissa nodded, speechless.

'We are in the process of making a fresh Treaty with His Highness about the mining of the diamonds. His Highness is as anxious as we are to increase the income from the industry. It is proposed to start another project on this land—if you would be agreeable to a mutually profitable arrangement.'

Suddenly, Melissa went cold at the prospect of being without her Koh-i-noor. It was the only home she had ever known!

'Should you decide to part with your property,' the Resident continued, 'you would become . . .' he paused significantly, 'one of the richest women in the country . . .'

But Melissa was barely listening. Her mind was filled with visions of her blossoming garden, of the fresh new paint on the outside of the house, of the cool, brilliant green stretches of newly planted lawn, of the flaming *gulmohar* tree now covered in fiery blooms, of the clear, clean waters of the river overhung by majestic teak and *saal* now in full leaf . . . all, all destroyed and trampled upon by the monster machines and the thousand pairs of feet that a mine would bring. It was a prospect that brought wrenching anguish to her heart but . . . could she bear to continue living here after all that had happened? Blind, raging anger shot through her as she realised just how thoroughly Gareth Caldwell had succeeded in disrupting the course of her entire life. He had laid to waste most brutally, so much that was precious to her. But then, she admitted to herself bitterly, it was nobody's fault but her own.

Outwardly, however, there was no sign of the storm within her heart as she faced Fred Carstairs with composure. 'Your suggestion takes me by surprise, Mr Carstairs. I . . . I have not given the matter any thought at all. Perhaps you would give me time to consider it?'

'Certainly, my dear, certainly,' he hastened to assure her. 'It is not a decision I expect you to make immediately.' He paused, his eyes speculative. 'You can inform me of your answer after your return from Metapilly.' He appeared to hover on the verge of asking a question, but changed his mind and took his leave.

It was a sad, sobering thought, the prospect of giving up her beloved home, her *only* home! But she could, somehow, no longer tolerate the idea of continuing to live in Altabad. Gareth Caldwell had seen to that! She would ask the Morrisons for advice. Perhaps she could purchase another property near them but then, John Morrison was a government servant and what would she do in Metapilly after they had left on transfer? In her dejection, she even considered the possibility of returning to England . . .

Arranging her clothes to be taken on the journey, late on Saturday night, Melissa found herself in the grip of an irritating apathy, unable to make up her mind about the smallest detail. She packed and unpacked, chopping and changing indecisively until even Zarina looked at her oddly. Finally, exasperated with herself, she slammed shut the lid of her trunk and dismissed Zarina for the night.

'I shall rise early and pack in the morning,' she said crossly. 'I don't seem to be able to put my mind to it now.'

She flounced off into the dressing room and set

about changing into her night clothes, and brushed her hair with slow, absent-minded strokes. Then, sighing heavily and feeling completely out of sorts, she returned to the bedroom—to halt in rigid shock.

Gareth Caldwell was sitting at her desk with his feet up on the top, swinging back and forth in the chair as if he had not a single care in the world!

Her breath caught in her throat as she clutched it with a chill hand and a million hammers pounded inside her heart. With a supreme effort, she gathered together her scattered wits and walked slowly into the room, pulling her flimsy robe closer around her.

'I see,' she said stiffly, 'that old habits die hard! I would like to remind you that my bedroom is no longer a public thoroughfare!'

He raised an eyebrow in surprise. 'Temper again?'

'Yes,' she snapped. She sat down slowly on the divan and faced him defiantly, hoping that he would not notice the tremble of her hands.

'Going away, I see.' He stood up and stretched lazily.

'Yes.'

'A sudden decision?'

'No.'

'May I ask why?'

'No, you may not! My comings and goings are no longer any concern of yours!' She rose and opened the bedroom door pointedly. 'Perhaps you would not object to leaving through normal channels? I feel you have compromised my reputation enough.'

He stared at her, rubbing his chin thoughtfully, then sauntered over to the open door. 'Aren't you even going to ask how I am?' he asked in tones of mock hurt.

'No. I can *see* how you are. If you're fit enough to go swinging up and down drainpipes,' she flung back heartlessly, 'then I have no doubt you are in no danger of imminent expiry! And now, I must ask you to leave. I don't wish to see you, *Captain* Caldwell, *ever again*!'

With a barely perceptible gesture, he stuck out a foot and slammed the door shut. Grasping her arm firmly, he pushed her back to the divan, then, with his hands on her shoulders, forced her to sit down. He towered above her with his hands on his hips and his mouth grim.

'*Now*,' he ground out, 'I am only too aware of what a silly little feather-brained *goose* you can be, but perhaps you would do me the honour of explaining this latest tantrum!'

'*I* don't owe *you* any explanations,' she stormed, furious with him. 'It is *you* who needs to explain your . . . your *flagrant* use of my services and the . . . the tissue of *lies* you have been spinning to me . . .'

'They were necessary,' he said quite calmly. 'However,' his voice took on a note of mockery, 'if you feel an apology is called for, then I apologise.'

'Your apology is not accepted!' she flung back at him, making an attempt to rise to her feet. Without seeming to move, he put out a hand and pushed her back on to the divan.

She stared at him appalled. 'How dare you barge into my bedroom uninvited and . . . and manhandle me like this, *Captain* Caldwell!' She was so angry that she had difficulty spitting out the words.

'Since we are to be quite formal, it's *Major* Caldwell,' he drawled, 'I received a well-deserved promotion two days ago.'

She ignored the information. 'In any case, what are you doing out of hospital when you were not meant to be discharged until Monday?'

'I discharged myself today—since I heard you are thinking of selling Koh-i-noor.'

'I am *not* th . . . in any case, what business is it of yours, what I do with my property?'

'None whatsoever,' he agreed quite pleasantly, 'and I'm not surprised. I've yet to meet a woman who wouldn't sell her soul for a handful of gold!'

'How *dare* you . . .' she gasped, spluttering with fury, 'You know I don't give a *hoot* for handfuls of gold . . .'

He looked very surprised. 'You mean,' he began raising an eyebrow, 'you would be willing to live on the meagre salary of a major in the Army?'

For a moment Melissa sat paralysed with shock, wondering if she had heard him correctly.

'It is impolite,' he said, lowering himself on to the divan next to her, 'to stare with your mouth open.'

'Wh-what did you s-say?' she stammered.

'I said, it is impolite to . . .'

'Gareth, be *serious*!' she exploded in frustrated exasperation, '*before* that . . .'

He laughed softly and put a finger under her chin. He kissed her very lightly, on the tip of her nose. 'You are,' he murmured, his tiger eyes full of a strange light, 'a very, very silly girl indeed. Why didn't you come to see me in hospital?'

'Why didn't you,' her eyes filled with slow tears,

'even bother to send me a letter? You seemed to have f-forgotten all about m-me . . .'

He put a hand on either side of her face. 'Because, you little numbskull, my right arm was in a bandage! You wouldn't have wanted me to dictate a love note to Mohan Das, now would you?'

For a moment she gaped. It was such a simple explanation, she had never even thought about it! '*Oh!*' she breathed faintly, feeling very foolish indeed.

He shook his head sadly, his hands still cupping her face. 'How can anyone as utterly *exquisite* as you,' he breathed with a soft laugh, 'have a brain as small as a *peanut!*' He brushed her lips with a kiss as light as a feather and she shuddered in excruciating ecstasy. 'You have the most devastating blue eyes I have ever gazed into. Do you know that?' he added.

'Flattery,' she gasped, determined not to give in so readily, 'will get you nowhere!'

'All right,' he asked easily, 'what will?'

'You had no *right* to . . . to mislead me so thoroughly and to make me do all those . . . *dreadful* things without telling me the truth . . .' Her lower lip began to tremble again. He gathered her very purposefully in his arms, forcing her to bury her face in his shoulder.

'I promise,' he whispered against her ear, 'that I will spend the rest of my life making restitution for everything that I have done but, for pity's sake, my dearest, most beloved Melissa, don't cry. I cannot *bear* to see tears in those beautiful, matchless eyes!'

'If all this is supposed to be a proposal of marriage,' she mumbled against his shirt, 'at least you could ask like a gentleman!' It was becoming increasingly difficult to stop the waves of exultation that flooded every nook and crevice of her body, making her limp with rapture.

He laughed softly. 'But you *will* marry me, won't you?'

'So that you can get your half share of Koh-i-noor?' she couldn't resist asking, even as her heart soared and her pulses throbbed with a bliss that was almost intoxicating.

'Hang Koh-i-noor!' Gareth roared suddenly, 'Hell and damnation to your Koh-i-noor! If you only knew how *sick* I am of your precious Koh-i-noor!'

'Then *why* do you want to marry me?' Good heavens, she moaned inwardly! Would he *never* say it?

'Because . . .' he paused fractionally.

'Because you love me to distraction?' she burst out impatiently.

'Of course I do, you must know that by now!'

'Then *say* it, *say* it!' she exclaimed, goaded beyond endurance. Oh, to hear him voice those precious, so long awaited words!

A lazy, languid smile hovered on his lips as his eyes shone with mellow gold lights. He held her so close that she could hardly breathe. He kissed her very slowly, very deeply and against her lips he murmured, so softly that the words barely reached her ears, 'I love you, my darling Missy, with all my heart . . . and in every way I know how . . .'

Melissa clung to him deliriously, trembling with overwhelming emotion. 'Oh, if you only knew, Gareth, how long I've waited to hear those words

. . .' Their lips met again and again, lingering against each other, reluctant to ever let go, until she gasped for breath and pushed him away gently.

'I thought you were in love with Maree Chandler . . .' she pouted in accusation.

Gareth sighed. '*More* explanations? Maree was a useful source of information, I told you that once.'

'What sort of information?' she persisted stubbornly, determined to cleanse the air between them of all future doubts.

He sighed again and released her for a moment. 'Is it all that important to know?' he asked, tilting his head to one side, his eyes holding a twinkle somewhere in the golden depths.

'Yes,' she said firmly. 'If you only knew how miserable I was about . . . about *that* . . .'

'Very well,' he sounded greatly amused. 'In spite of her rather . . . splendid appearance, Maree is basically a very stupid woman! Even more so than . . .' he kissed her very swiftly to confirm that he was only teasing, '. . . than you. Without realising it, in casual coversation she used to provide a good deal of information about what was happening at the mines every day. Some of that information proved very useful indeed in planning when and how to "steal" the diamonds.'

'And that was all?' Melissa asked suspiciously. 'What about . . . ?'

Gareth placed a very firm finger on her lips. 'Roy Chandler is a friend of mine,' he said quietly, 'I may have used his delectable wife to ferret out information about the mines but—in spite of what Altabad gossip might have you believe—*that is all*! And now,' his lips set grimly, 'if you ever so much as *mention* Maree Chandler to me again, I shall put you across my knees and spank the daylights out of you! *Is that clear?*'

She lowered her eyes meekly, her cup of joy now well and truly full. 'Yes, Gareth,' she whispered in a small voice, looking so totally appealing that he was forced to take her in his arms again and kiss her soundly.

'Maree Chandler is in the past. What matters is the future,' he whispered in her ear, '*our* future together, maybe even here at Koh-i-noor . . .'

'*Here?*' Her heart bounded excitedly. 'But I heard you may be posted elsewhere . . . ?'

'Yes, that was a possibility, but His Highness has requested Calcutta to send me back to Altabad as his Chief Adviser. Fred Carstairs tells me they are considering the request very seriously at headquarters. You would like to stay on at Koh-i-noor, wouldn't you darling?'

'Oh *yes*,' Melissa breathed, her eyes alive with a dazzling radiance. 'I never want to leave Koh-i-noor . . . as long as you are with me . . .'

'But you were thinking of selling out, now weren't you?'

'No!' she protested, 'I was not! But . . .' her face became thoughtful, 'I was considering . . . the mining of the diamonds brings in good revenue for the Maharaja to help better the lot of his people. And this is a very vast estate, isn't it? Do you think we require so much land, Gareth, for just two of us?'

'No,' he said, smiling broadly, '*I* certainly don't. I would be more than content with enough land to hold a reasonably sized four-poster bed . . .'

She blushed and pushed him away, pretending to be cross. 'Do be serious for a while, Gareth, there is something that needs to be resolved . . .'

He sighed resignedly. 'All right, my stubborn little Missy. Speak on. I am at your service entirely.'

'I have been thinking . . . there is so much land on the other side of the river. It is uncultivated with not much foliage or splendid old trees. We cannot even see it from the house so the activity would constitute no irritation to us . . .'

Gareth's eyes narrowed. 'You would sell part of your land for a diamond mine?'

Melissa's eyes widened in horror. 'Oh *no*! I would not dream of taking money for it! Koh-i-noor is mine not by right but only because of the generosity of His Highness. I would only be returning to him what is his. It would be a small gesture on my part of gratitude for the untold riches he has brought into my life in terms of happiness and . . . and your love . . .' She paused and bit her lip shyly.

Gareth's face lit up with a smile of infinite pride and tenderness. Very purposefully he encircled her with his arms, covering her face with kisses. 'You are,' he breathed, 'a very exceptional woman, Melissa Castlewood, do you know that? Had you talked in terms of money, I would have . . . ,' he paused and frowned.

'You would have?' she asked impudently.

'I would have put you across my knees, rump side up, and treated you to the wrong end of a frying pan!'

'You would not have dared!' she giggled snuggling against his heartbeat contentedly. 'I really do think . . .'

He stopped her mouth with a kiss. 'The trouble

with you is, my darling, that you think far more than is called for. From now on,' he said severely, 'you will leave the thinking to me. Is that understood?'

'And what do you expect *me* to do—restrict myself to preparing your lordship's breakfast and bath-water?'

'Yes, that too. But far more important—I expect you, my beloved little Missy, to fill your Koh-i-noor with dozens of tiny Caldwells, that's what!' He laughed as she hid her scarlet face in his shoulder. 'That should keep you out of trouble for the time being.' He laughed again and ruffled her hair tender-ly.

She started as a sudden thought struck her. 'Oh dear! I am expected in Metapilly tomorrow after-noon . . .'

'No you're not,' he retorted complacently. 'I've already sent a message to the Morrisons telling them that you have been . . . er . . . unavoidably de-tained . . .'

'Oh.' She frowned at him. 'You are very sure of yourself, aren't you, Gareth Caldwell?' she asked, annoyed.

'No, my dearest one,' he whispered lovingly, 'It is *you* I am very sure of . . .'

After which, of course, there was very little left to be said.

A very special gift for Mother's Day

You love Mills & Boon romances. Your mother will love this attractive Mother's Day gift pack. First time in paperback, four superb romances by leading authors. A very special gift for Mother's Day.

United Kingdom £4.40

On sale from 24th Feb 1984

A Grand Illusion
Maura McGiveny

Sensual Encounter
Carole Mortimer

Desire in the Desert
Mary Lyons

Aquamarine
Madeleine Ker

Look for this gift pack where you buy
Mills & Boon romances.